Preface:

The last op-ed piece from the Wall Street Journal, dated July 4, 2020.

The United States is beyond repair from what the Founding Fathers had designed it to be back on September 17, 1787. The shambles caused by man's greed to be self absorbed, and find the easier route has left most void of any understanding of the true value of freedom.

Freedom is not easy, and cannot be kept by words alone. It is a state of mind, and its ways are something you live and breathe. No, freedom isn't always rich or rewarding because it requires much work. It requires passion, and commitment to its true meaning.

With the newly elected President Redman we shall never see another election that is run based upon the concepts of our constitution, and the limited scope that government should serve in. For he is a President in title only, not subject to constitutional laws and procedures—he is a machine that has a ruthless heart and a determination to remain in a position of power.

We no longer have a government for the people; it is one for itself. It is the big Machine that keeps growing and stomping out all that defies it. Our elected officials have become nothing more than a namesake, like the Kings and Queens of England that we left behind so many decades ago. Their positions and promises are meaningless words because they cannot say what they truly desire—to have more power and money—things that you give them by bestowing faith in their corrupt ways.

All that has happened has left people with one decision to make. Are they going to hop on board the Machine and hope to gain from the misery of those who cherish true freedom, or are they going to be the ones who stand up and make a difference. Even a speck of sand can change the tides of a mighty river.

For my fellow American's who have kept their constitutional mindset despite the madness, I implore you to be the Rogue Spartan we need in order to change things. It will not be easy, and it will involve full out rebellion against the Machine; plus a determined ferocity to take down what has stolen so much from each and every one of us. Please know that if you die it will be for freedom, and not for an authoritarian government who cares not for you. If you succeed, you will be given the most challenging task ever—getting mankind to believe in the power of true freedom once again.

As I write these last words, and put them into print I may never be heard from again. Please know that my consequences are not of concern to me, but my words inspiring action are what truly matter. My friends, be inspired.

Dr. Jay Secton
Constitutionalist

These words are seared into the minds of many, and considered the most powerful words ever written aside from the Constitution. They came from a man who valued freedom above all else. You see, America had become a place where freedoms had slowly been taken away in lieu of individuals expectations of what they could receive without contributing anything in the way of moral character, or selfless acts. Dr. Jay Secton, the man who dared put his opinion into well thought out written words, was sentenced to a life of servitude in a prison camp as a result. The Machine thought they quieted him by isolating him, but the words he spoke made him a hero of cult-like proportions. To this day, many await for the right person to help bring his words to life, and act upon what he requested so eloquently that 4th of July, 2020.

Chapter One: May 22, 2042

One would have thought with all the incessant regulations from the EPA of long ago, and the new EGA (Environmental Governance Agenda), which was basically like the EPA on steroids, would have stopped all of the pollution in the air, and we'd all be breathing air so clean that we lived to be a hundred—which would completely suck in this world by the way; however, that was definitely not the case. The evidence lie in the visuals of blanketing smog, pollutants in the air, and the garbage lining the city streets. You see, New York City only allows a certain few government officials to have vehicles because of the "importance of their time". The rest of us, people like me, always have and always will ride the bus if we want to get anywhere at all—unless it's outside the city limits—which are off limits without the expressed written permission of the Boundary Exceptions Approval Division. Yah, I know, asinine laws from a bunch of ass-munchers.

I'm sitting on this uncomfortable metal bench waiting for the bus, which is running late as usual. Maybe it's another hold-up, or someone shot the driver again. That seems to happen about once a week in this city, usually within about twenty feet of one of the armed MCU (Militant Command Unit) that walks around protecting us. You can't miss them. They're huge beasts, seemingly half man and half ox. The orange bands they were around their arms to identify themselves are likely bigger than my head. And using the word protection to describe what they do is a fairly far cry from reality. True protection usually costs you money, money that most of us can't afford to part with or just refuse to pay the MCU. The Machine can't strip away the things you carry with you in their heart, although they certainly try.

My eyes avert over to a lamppost that is about five feet away. Some prick is mugging this guy, and there isn't a damn thing he can do to stop it. The MCU guy walks by, and the mugger tosses him a twenty spot, and that's it. He keeps on going because he received his fee to turn away. I shake my head. I've been mugged three times now, and I've found that by trying to blend in and remain anonymous my chances of being avoided raise considerably. It may seem cowardly to some, but it makes sense to me. I'm not exactly known for muscles, brawn, and cocky talk. Avoidance equals survival, and while this world may not be fantastic I am still a fan of being alive. Another good policy I've learned is never to carry more than a ten spot on you at any given time. All the thieves seem to have an innate ability to smell money on people so if you don't have it, well that makes you a bit less stinky to them.

The latest mugging victim is interesting to me. He carries himself differently. I can hear him spouting off a colorful array of words to the mugger, who just turns around and flips him off as he goes on his way. He has some balls. That guy could be armed with some makeshift shank that he whipped up while spending a night in the local jail. You just never know, and honestly there is nothing that would be considered shocking any more. The United States has gone to hell, and it'd under the command of our supposed President, Redman. Ever since 2020, our President is not really elected, but he's arrogant enough to like the title so he keeps it. Even in today's environment he probably couldn't get away with Dictator.

I watch as the guy who got mugged sits down next to me, and I briefly nod, not wishing to get involved in any trouble his mouth might get him into.

"Hey man, did you see that? What a pansy piece of crap that guy was. Oh well, he didn't get much."

I smile and nod, not ready to chat with this dude at all. He just keeps on talking. "My name is Felix, nice to meet ya'. Don't blame you for not stepping in. You're pretty scrawny."

Okay, I can't help but look now. "Hey, I'm Ben." I turn back away.

"Ben, I should have pounded the hair right off that dipshit's ass. What a prick he was."

"Why didn't you?"

"Ah, it seemed a waste of time since I was carrying a counterfeit twenty. Let him get his balls screwed to the wall when he tries to pass that off on someone. That MCU dude is probably in hot pursuit already. Probably tried to go get him some lovin' down a back alley, and got pummeled by a pimp. Classic."

"I'm not really sure what to say about that...Felix. My entire goal each and every day is just to make it through work, get home, hang out with my dog Otto, and do what

I do out of the sight of all the raging lunatics out here on the streets."

"Dismal, aren't you? Out of curiosity, am I one of those raging lunatics?"

"Still weighing in on that."

"I like you. You ever go out, and live it up?"

"Nah, my friends and I like to hang out at home, and stay away from the fray."

"Fray, funny you should mention that. It's the name of the little underground club I like to frequent. Pretty close to hear actually. Just under the GSB (Government Stability Bureau) office—ironic twist because we unleash all we got at the club, and it's not too stable either. We get buck ass wild."

"Aren't you afraid of the MCU taking you away somewhere, and you'll end up fading into oblivion?" I couldn't help but ask. What this Felix guy spoke of was so out of the realm of what my friends and I would do, except maybe Max.

"My friend, you can't always worry about the consequences. Sometimes you just need to get inspired and go for it. That's what I do."

"Dr. Jay Secton," I say. Those are words that only those who follow the great Constitutionalist would dare echo to a stranger.

"Definitely inspired by that guy. He had more umph in him than a guy working ladies night."

"What's ladies night?"

"Something they used to have back in the day."

"Why did you say he *had* more umph? Think he's dead?"

"Who knows. Being locked up in one of those camps is about as close as you can get. I'd rather be dead than live in a place like that."

I am feeling emboldened by the forthright Felix, and ask, "How do you know that? Have you ever been in one?"

"Just the outside looking in. Helped bust a friend out once. I had to die my hair blonde for a year and gain like fifty freakin' pounds to cover my identity. Lived off the streets, and under the radar."

"How'd you manage that?"

"It was not easy. These current authoritarian fuckheads have their slimy little ways weaseled into everything. Staying fat when you're broke, have no food, and can't go home is not easy."

"Did they do anything to your parents?"

"No. My dad works for the Machine, and he wouldn't have thought twice about turning me in for a nice bonus if I was found. He's a real dick, my old man. Your old man a dick?"

"Unfortunately my parents passed away in a subway accident. The tracks were in disrepair and their car plummeted off the side."

"That sucks."

"Yah, it does." I look up and saw my bus, Transit Line 5, pulling up. "Well, this is my ride. Hang in there, and hopefully all goes well for you."

"You too. Remember, if you feel like getting a little freaky come on down to Fray anytime. Tell them that Felix invited you, and they'll treat you like royalty after a thorough cavity search."

I think my jaw drops, and I certainly can't say a word. Felix lets me off the hook. "Just kidding."

"Okay, I'll remember you if I'm ever in the mood to get buck ass wild, as you put it," I say, and then I walk on to the bus, and take my usual seat right up front. I like it that way because I don't have to deal with looking at anyone, and can hop off the bus as soon as it stops in front of

TerraCorp, the employer that pays me just enough to be able to live without any roommates, and keep feeding my Chihuahua Otto, who eats more like a cow than a little dog.

The half hour bus ride to work goes surprisingly fast because I am thinking about Felix. You didn't meet characters like that every day. He is memorable, and his long thick sandy brown hair and tattooed body made him really stand apart. He must be fairly tough too because tattoos, aside the government issued numbers that they placed on your back left shoulder blade, have been banned for about twenty years. I like to think of my tattoo as my alter ego, Citizen Number 20571289, which basically means that I am the 1289th person born on May 7, 2020. I wonder how old Felix may be, and it's hard to say. He can't be any more than ten years older than me, and I just turned twenty-two a week ago.

The bus screeches to a stop in front of TerraCorp, letting out a big puff of black smoke from its exhaust system. I jump up, and prepare to enter the building that I have been entering six days a week since turning eighteen, and was approved to take the computer vocation classes, which granted me permission to use the Intranet. I have never taken a vacation, left New York City, or missed work other than ten days when I had the flu so bad that I thought I was going to die. Apparently TerraCorp took it seriously too because I'd been at work when I started shaking and vomiting all over, eventually fainting into my own puke. I still have not lived that down from my co-workers. It is one of only a handful of interesting things that happened in an otherwise dreary world that made black and gray look exciting.

I walk into work and sling off my backpack, plopping it under my desk, and start to do my thing. I am in charge of monitoring the Intranet usage of various companies, ensuring that no one is breaking the laws or posting things that are considered against the Government, and their resolve to make the United States a fair place. On days when I find a violator it is like hitting the jackpot, which is now considered a free year's salary in exchange for a sappy testimonial of how amazing President Redman is. Yes, my job is lame, but if I just do my thing without causing a ruckus, and go home I will be okay. Truthfully, it is the benefits that come with having access to the Intranet that really pay off. It is my hobby, and it is all consuming.

Eight hours later, I am walking out of TerraCorp, and on my way home for the night. It is only Monday, and I cannot wait for the weekend, and to get together with Max, Cal, and Amy. It always proves to be interesting, and the three of them managed to make me feel that I am not quite so shy, and socially awkward. You could best summarize us as four smart rebel geeks that *really* get into our hobby, making it a battle of wits and wise cracks against each other. Admittedly, I am better at the wits than the wisecracks.

Chapter Two: May 27, 2042

"Okay everyone, let's make tonight's challenge about who can get into the deepest layer of security in ten minutes." Max slaps his hands together, and shouts out a big "Hoo-fuckin-rah". His spiked blonde hair is half flattened from just waking up, and you can still see the crease in the side of his face. Max works nights, monitoring the city sewer problems, which seem to be prevalent as of late. Little does the city know that those problems exist because Max is always planting a virus into them, which just happens to make one of the programs misfire, and send stench wafting into the vents of the most expensive houses in the city. That is his thing, and he loves it.

"Seriously Max? How many shit bombs can you send out there? Let's do something a bit more challenging," Amy says. She isn't impressed with Max's impish charm, and tells him he is a first class dink-master at least once an hour on hacking nights. The problem is that when she says it everyone always cracks up because she sounds so serious, and even creases her brow in a serious manner. The more people laugh the more her green eyes spark. Truth be told, any one of us guys would gladly accept more from her because she is smart, and pretty cool despite being so serious. So far, she has not offered anyone anything aside from computer advice though. "I say that we each target one thing, and find out a secret about it. As for me, I'm targeting the MCU, and want to get information on the lasers that they are using for those new guns—the ones that will pulverize you in a second flat, sending you crumbling in a pile of ashes."

"Well, we should have time to do both of those things," I offer.

"Ben, always the peace maker, aren't you? When you going to go a little crazy?" Max asks.

"When you go a little mellow," Cal says for me. Cal is all about conspiracy and figuring out what the government is up to and he is rather brilliant at doing it without us getting busted. One time we had a close call and we were alerted that the ITC (Intranet Tribunal Committee) thugs were on the way, and Max scrambled the stoplights while Cal erased our cyber fingerprints. Amy and I quickly hauled all our computers into the "safety zone". That was an old laundry chute in the apartment building we all lived in. It was made of such thick metal that it couldn't be detected by the sensory device that the ITC prided itself on. What their pride had failed to acknowledge was that the guy who engineered the technology released it to a few select people who knew how to deal in those matters. It was the Secton followers hopes that one of those people would turn out to be the leader of the anti-Machine movement. That person was called the Rogue Spartan, and Secton wrote about it twenty some years prior. So far the Machine had been wrong, and they'd also been stupid. Eliminating those the Machine labeled traitors did not eliminate the problem. Cal had intercepted the message to show us how to work with the technology, and we'd all learned as much as we could from it, salivating at our ability to beat the Machine. It was a hacking high, and we were tripping on it whenever we could safely do it. One thing that we all agreed on was that it would be pretty cool to be the rogue that crumbled the Machine. Those conversations never took place outside of hacking night, and they kind of fueled our hacking dreams, keeping us going.

"I'm just going to do both, and you guys do whatever you want," I finally say. I breathe out, and my exhale causes my curly bangs to flutter in the air. It is a habit that I have when I am hacking, as it helps me focus and stay relaxed. Then I pick up Otto, who always sits on my lap when I am hacking, and get ready to begin. Unlike my friends, I prefer being quiet when I hack, and don't like to talk at the same time. I really don't know how they do it, but they all can—just not me. *Okay, I occasionally mumbled to Otto, but he can't talk back.* However, when something needs to be said I don't hesitate; like that time when Max was going to break into the City Commissioner's office to erase the records of all the "juvenilely distressed", a new term that the Machine started using for anyone under eighteen who didn't comply with their agenda. It was highly likely that the acts of some of the Machine's leaders could also be considered "juvenilely distressed", and all their kids could be on the list too if they didn't come from privilege. For the most part the Machine's leaders are self indulgent bozos who never had to grow up because they bought into the hype. We called it Redmanitized, and it is not considered a compliment.

My idea wins out…one of the benefits of not always talking. We are doing both hacking challenges. Then a symphony of fast typing fingers starts to sound out, and we are all racing to get to the deepest layer in ten minutes, Cal ends up winning, getting the dubious honor of claiming next week's challenge as a result. We don't have actual cash to bet so we do the best we can with various antes, and winning is definitely a good thing. All of us are pretty safe when either myself, Cal, or Amy win. It is when Max wins that you have to worry. *Max and that Felix guy I met at the bus stop would get along infamously.*

Max pulls out a cigar to offer it as a celebration, and we all panic. He cracks up, knowing that he's gotten us just like he wanted to. Thankfully Max is not so bold as to smoke in the apartment because the detectors that are required to be in everyone's housing works in conjunction with the GSB. If they caught you smoking you'd receive a $1,000.00 air contamination fine, be required to take a twenty hour community class on the dangers of illegal and dangerous activity, plus be relocated to a place that is called the Government Watch Housing Project. *Everything the Machine touches lets you know it…Government this, Government that, screw Government.* And if you can't pay the fine or don't oblige with the to-do list you are sent to a work camp for five years. The jobs suck ass from what we all hear too.

The next challenge is secrets, and all of our faces light up. It is definitely the common bond, and the one that makes us feel we have an edge in the madness of the lives we all live.

"Otto, we've got this one boy," I say, petting his head.

"Oooh, watch out. Ben's talking to Otto tonight—that means serious business," Max chides. Even Amy laughs. Yah, I get a lot of crap for talking to my dog, but truthfully, I don't care and I won't be stopping the habit any time soon. Otto is my only living family, an orphan like me. It was a really great day when I found him whimpering in a corner, so hungry. I immediately took him on as my own, and paid the big fees that come with the luxury of pet ownership. It took me a bit to save them up though, and I had to hide him in my apartment. The one benefit from that is that to this day he can take care of his business just by me holding him over the toilet. It's an awkward sight, but it makes life with a dog in an apartment considerably easier.

All right. We are all set to go, and discover some secrets. As Amy had mentioned, she was going to search for information on the newest MCU weapons that were made for terrorizing civilians from a safe distance. Those weapons were also said to have the ability for Redman to shut them down at will if he thought he was in danger due to any sort of rebellious act.

Cal is ready to find out the latest people that the Government is targeting for shutdown and takeover. The Machine runs a tight ship with private enterprise, and one mistake—even flushing the toilet too many times—can be cause for turning it over to government control. Naturally, that is their ultimate goal and one of the only things that the Machine is efficient at.

Max is going to put the City Commissioner's daughter on the Sterilization Consideration List. His is an act of revenge because he did hit on her about three years ago, and she told him he was hardly the caliber of person she could ever consider a relationship with. We'd all been there and laughed about it. In reflection, I actually think it may have been one of those rare times where Max's feelings were genuinely hurt. He is a good guy even if he cherishes being obnoxious on a daily basis.

I am going mellow tonight, hoping that I'd be able to find my work review and see what is in store for my future. I don't love TerraCorp by any means, but I want to do more than what I am currently doing. I have to hide my skills somewhat so people won't be suspect of what I really can do on a computer. I have done that pretty well, and built my skills at an appropriate speed that will hopefully leave me unsuspecting in the eyes of TerraCorp's leadership. They don't really appreciate being outshined by an employee, especially a Tier 3 one like me. *What type of world forces you to hide who you are, not letting your true potential show? That could only be acceptable in a messed up world. I guess that's the answer.*

It doesn't take me long to find my review. It is pathetic, but it appeases my mind. They don't really say anything at all, just ramble on with all the jargon and lingo that is suggested for such reviews. I show potential, I could be a bit more outgoing with peers, and I am a valued part of the workforce. Last year my review said the same things, just in a different order. The upside is that they don't suspect I am capable of doing anything outside the limits of acceptability.

I move over to see what Amy is doing, and watch her go in layer after layer, pausing on occasion to scribble notes, but mostly relying on her excellent memory to absorb what she reads. The weapons information is insane, and Amy looks up at me, smiling. "I see weaknesses in this."

We'd all developed photographic memories to support our hacking skills. It is the best way to be fast, efficient, and remember everything we come across that we feel is worth remembering. We have even started creating an e-binder with all that we'd learned about the Machine. We call it SOURCE (Secrets Outted Under R Computer Expertise). The four e-binders are actually flash drives that looked like an earring, and can be worn. That makes it easier for us to hide them, and keep them on our beings at all times. The devices had set us back every bit of savings we had at the time because they had needed to be purchased on the black market, and off the radar. The guy who'd made them didn't want to be known by anyone, and preferred keeping his skills hidden—like us. I hadn't went that night, only Max. He came back grinning, telling us that he'd threatened to put that guy on the Treason Suspect List if he mentioned the purchase to anyone. He really was a dick sometimes, and we all knew it was a small miracle that he'd make it back intact, and had not been roughed up by someone that he pissed off just a bit too much.

Since Redman has come into office, the Government has a big agenda of making sure no one group had too much information or power. It is their replacement for the Checks & Balances System that used to be a part of the Legislature. If anyone ever truly feels secure or confident, including Redman himself, it would be very shocking for me to hear about or believe. The ones who do tend to be the ones who usually mess up, and disappear in the night and are never heard from again. SOURCE is our way to keep what we'd learned in case something would ever happen to any of us, which could be as easy as being told we had to relocate to another city, or getting into trouble. We had each other's backs and that was the most absolute thing in all our lives.

"Wow. TerraCorp is on this list," Cal blurts out. That catches my attention.

I stand up and go walk over, standing behind him. "They're being targeted for government take-over, and shutdown." Cal is typing away, and talking animatedly.

"Why?"

"It says Reason 39.8(c)-1, and Reason 12.6(b)-5. Let's see…the reasons state: high amounts of computer activity at unusual times, and failed efforts to enter websites that are government related, and not necessary to the company's mission."

"Someone's trying to hack from TerraCorp? I wonder who. That is pretty risky. The bosses patrol our cubicles they like they are the MCU themselves."

"I don't know, but it would be good to find out. If anything, that person may have something of value for us," Cal says.

"Like what?" Amy asks.

"Who knows. If they're good they have probably erased as much of their cyber presence as they've left behind. It only takes one trace to be discovered—DNA of the cyber world."

"Man that would suck. I don't like the thought of that at all," I comment.

"Why are you worried, Ben? You are as squeaky clean as they come. You are quiet, which makes the Machine think you've brought into their plan. You go through painful measures to not upset the flow of anything, which means the Machine thinks you are one of their little robots. And, I could keep going on and on. Don't worry so much." Max folds his hands above his head, and leans back, staring at me.

Otto looks at him and gives a little growl. He doesn't care for Max for some unknown reason. "You're probably right," I say.

I turn to Cal and realize that he has already signed off the computer and is starting his scramble. "Ben, I'm going to need you to do something…something that you can only do from a computer in TerraCorp, not externally."

"What is that?" I ask slowly, instantly nervous about what it could be.

"I'm going to write down some sequences, passwords, and information for you. They should be able to get you into the mainframe of TerraCorp's internal network. I want you to find out who has been trying to enter into the system. It should take you only ten minutes maximum. You'll have to determine the safest time."

"Why? That seems like a stupid risk. What if I get busted and they think it's been me? I'll be screwed."

"You'll be fine. It's your call, Ben, but it is in your best interests to know who is doing that, and give them some time to get out of there before they're discovered. Plus, you don't want to work directly for the Machine, do you?"

"Fine, I'll do it." The threat of working directly for the Machine is enough to make all of us act, even when we'd rather not. Let's just say that it is not an option any of us would ever consider.

Chapter Three: May 30, 2042

I am watching through my peripheral vision as my manager walks past. From years of experience, I realize that one goes past me every twenty minutes like clockwork. It's always been that way, and they all think we are oblivious to the fact, but all of us workers know. How could you not unless you were a moron, in which case you wouldn't be working at TerraCorp.

Fred, the guy who sits next to me keeps talking, and wanting my attention. "Fred, I'm on to something right here. I need some quiet please." I realize that I'm whispering more quietly than usual.

"Oh sure. No problem, man. What is it?"

I don't answer, and the silence finally gives him the hint to shut the hell up. I realize that I'm blowing out and my curly bang is gently flapping up and down. I try not to do that at work in case anyone has seen the habit, and knows that it means I'm really focusing on something. No need to draw attention to what I may deem as serious, which is definitely what this task from Cal is.

I'm into the mainframe, and getting closer to the users patterns, and searches. It's hard to narrow things down, and my heart skips a beat when I see my name, with number 20571289 next to it. It says that I'm on an internal layer, and the letter U is next to it. U means unauthorized, and I know that I only have a brief amount of time left, and had better hope that no one higher up is in this part of the system and sees my name.

As I scroll down the names one does stand out to me. It's Mr. Fairabee, the Human Resources Coordinator. Why would he need to do anything at all, except maybe…I stop, instinctually realizing that ten minutes has passed, and quickly log out, switching to a screen for a company that sells cleaning solutions.

"Mr. Danrick, could I have a word with you?"

I whip my head around, and see Mr. Richards standing there. This is surprising, and my stomach sinks. He's the VP of TerraCorp, and prior to right now he has never spoken to me one time, and I would have never thought he'd know my name.

My mind is whirling with thoughts, and I'm trying to stay relaxed looking, and not show that I am nervous. I get up and follow him to his office, which is up two floors. I put my hands in my pants pockets, trying to look casual, but I'm really wiping the sweat from them. I don't say a word, and either does Mr. Richards.

We enter his office, and he shuts the door behind him. "Have a seat, Ben."

"What…what's this about, sir?"

"Oh please call me Mr. Richards."

"Okay, Mr. Richards, what's this about?"

"I think you've been leaving a few skills off your resume. What do you think?"

"I…uh…I…"

"I'll let you off the hook, Ben. I know that you've just entered into our TerraCorp mainframe, and have been searching out some information. Would you like to tell me why?"

I pause. Do I tell him the truth? No, because that would get others in trouble, and I'd still be in hot water anyways. "I don't know what you mean, Mr. Richards."

"I know you do. Let me put your mind at ease first, Ben. I am willing to overlook your activity, and that's a good thing for you. It means I won't be calling the Intranet Tribunal Commission, and turning you in. However, this kindness does have certain expectations."

"Like what?"

"I want you to use your skills to get information for me. I will pay you handsomely for it, and keep the authorities off your case. I'd caution you though, if you get sloppy or share what I am requesting there will be nothing I'd be able to do to protect you."

"You want me to hack for you?"

"I prefer something more dignified than hacking, for that's a young person's sport that doesn't do much to lead or inspire people. Let's call what you are going to do for me information retrieval, and that should work just fine. Agree?"

"Agree." *What the hell is going on?*

"I will deliver you messages as need be, and you'll be expected to get information back to me within forty-eight hours of doing so. Don't try to incorporate any help either, such as that of your rather resourceful friends. This is our deal, and not to be shared."

"Okay Mr. Richards."

"Now, why don't you go back to work, and focus on what you are getting paid to do at TerraCorp. You'll be able to focus on what I'm going to pay you to do later. I'll give you your first assignment at end of day."

I hurry out of Mr. Richards' office, my heart racing and thumping. My head feels like it is going to explode. I rush into the men's bathroom, and lean over, hurling into the toilet, and breaking out into a cold sweat.

That was close, but I can't help but wonder why I'd been given the opportunity to get paid for hacking—rather information retrieval—by Mr. Richards. It doesn't make sense. *It's better than dealing with the ITC, so just wait and see. If you don't, you're screwed.*

I go back to work at my cube, and notice everyone looking at me. Their faces give them away and they are all curious about what Mr. Richards had wanted. Fred doesn't hesitate to ask, and I just reply that it is private— none of his business. I sound snappy, but I don't care. I just don't need him talking incessantly to me. There is suddenly a lot of heavy shit going through my mind, and I need to sort it all out.

At day's end when I am finally heading home, Mr. Richards gets on the elevator with me. He doesn't say a word, and I don't either. Once we leave the TerraCorp building he hands me a small drive. "Here's your task, Mr. Danrick. I look forward to your results."

Chapter Four: June 21, 2042

Helping Mr. Richards is both rewarding and nerve-racking. It's interesting knowing that I have a free pass to explore into parts of the Intranet that I shouldn't be in, and that I can pull it off. The extra money is certainly good, and in just a few short weeks I've made enough extra to actually save some. I'm hoping to buy some technology. The nerve-racking part of helping Mr. Richards comes from that slight fear of getting busted by the wrong people, and by keeping secrets from Amy, Max, and Cal.

My suddenly extra busy schedule, and having to drop hacking night for three weeks straight has left everyone annoyed at me, and questioning me. I'm not a very good liar, and every time someone approaches me about what's going on, I can tell that I get all twitchy and start to sweat. Amy is the worse.

"Ben, what is going on? I can tell you're hiding something. What is it?"

"Amy, it's nothing okay. I'm just getting a little bored with the hacking thing, and taking a break. That's all." I realize that I'm petting Otto's little head fervently, and let up on it.

"You-are-full-of-shit," Amy says, offering me no reprieve at all. Yes, she's right, but damn it, I cannot tell or there are going to be four people minimum that are in some instant trouble that cannot be gotten out of easily, if at all. I have to protect them. I know I have to up my game, and show some determination so they don't continue busting my balls trying to get me to crack and reveal information.

"So what if I am full of shit? Why do I have to tell you guys everything that is going on?"

"Because we're your friends, Ben."

"Well, as my friends, I'd appreciate it if you stopped harassing me, and please share that message with Cal and Max."

"Max is set to put you on one of his lame-ass lists. He's getting annoyed, being bugged by his own curiosity of what you're holding from him." One thing I hadn't thought of thus far is my friends possibly hacking me. They could surely do it, and that would suck. Or would it? Maybe that'd be a way to let them know what's going on without saying a word. Something to think about...later.

I put my hands on my head, going back to the more immediate threat of Max's fury. Knowing Max it's probably one of those lists where they'll swoop down on me at work and scare the piss out of me. Amy is right when she calls him a dink-master. "Look Amy, I just can't tell you, but I am fine. Trust me."

"Not leaving me much of a choice."

"Just please do it. Look, I've got to get back to work. Sorry about that, but I'm going to have to ask you to go."

Amy frowns at me, and does something strange. She gives me a hug, and it's kind of tight. She really is worried about me. Man, this fucking sucks...I don't like worrying my friends like this. I'd love to tell them what's going on. We could make a real hauling financially, and information wise, if we could all do this together. As it is,

I'd never realized how much each of them had taught me about their various specialties through the past years. It's made my projects for Mr. Richards considerably easier.

As soon as Amy walks out the door I breathe a huge sigh of relief. My weekend assignment was sitting on my kitchen table, and I'd barely managed to hide it below my backpack before she came into through the apartment. Since neither I nor my friends have much of a social life we've all kind of developed this open door policy about visiting. It hasn't been a big deal until now. Now I have to start locking my door, and it'll likely be the last straw for Max, and Cal especially, maybe Amy too. What choice do I have?

The companies and individuals that Mr. Richards has me research are all so random that I'm having a tough time getting the connection between them. There has to be something, and I plan on finding out when I get some free time. I'll put together a lay-out of all the companies, and then try to make some sense of it. It would be awesome to find out what he's up to without him realizing it. I can't say why for certain, but I feel that having some clout against him is a good thing. After all, I'm completely at his mercy, and it's not like he really cares about me. He certainly has no reason to be loyal to me. The time will come when his use for me is done, and then what? I don't like thinking about that, but I do seriously need to consider it. Maybe I should save my money from Mr. Richards in case I need to find me a good attorney at some point. *Yah right, attorney's are the biggest pawns*

out there for the Machine's agenda, despite being labeled
private sector.

The information that I've found out so far is quite
fascinating, and I can't focus on the new project at this
moment so I start to write down the basics of each search.
The details are many pages long, and while I had to put
them on paper for Mr. Richards I was also able to
memorize them for myself.

1. Federal Actuary Thomas Barnes has found a
   way to funnel money out of the official
   Government retirement accounts, and has sent
   it to a Dr. Martin Stethson.

2. Virilian Industries, a medical research group
   that specializes in contagions, has recently
   received an influx of generous donations
   which have been designated toward a chemical
   weapon that would be used to "control the
   masses" according to the general case briefing.
   Dr. Martin Stethson is on Virilian's Board of
   Directors, and recently proposed that Virilian
   be half owned by the Machine.

3. LaserMachination was recently issued a Cease
   and Desist Operations Order by the MCU
   Grand Chief, Colonel Filas Redman, brother of
   President Redman. The tip came from
   someone who believes to be an anonymous
   source, but is known to be Cecil Dantworth.
   He is actually a former TerraCorp employee

who now serves in the position of Ambassador of Right Acts for President Redman.

There are about four other things on my list, but one thing that clearly shows is that Redman is involved in everything he can be, Redmanitizing people into doing his dirty work for him, and giving him more power on a daily basis in sneaky ways. Of course, there is no longer any true media, and the state run propaganda machines are loaded with rosy stories of the Machine is helping young children, and elderly people across America. If you fell anywhere in between you were screwed, and dispensable. Children were the way of the future. Old people who made it most likely submitted to the Machine, or could do a heck of an acting job. The thought of me and my friends having to put up a facade and act until our dying days was enough motive for me to just go out there and get all crazy on someone. Well, the thought was nice, but my personality definitely didn't have even a sprinkling of irrational behavior in it. It didn't bother me because that was just me, not the Machine.

I found myself plugging away at data bases, and clearing deep access levels until about three in the morning. Thankfully I didn't have to go to work that Saturday, something that Mr. Richards had waived me from having to do once I started taking on his tasks. It had raised plenty of suspicion with my co-workers too, most of them thinking I was some kiss ass sucking his dick—or so the one note tossed on my desk said. Harsh. I suppose I'd be suspicious too if I were watching me from a distance.

For the next weeks I grew more isolated, not having anyone to talk to. Cal, Max, and Amy had just stopped coming by or bothering. The locked door had been the last straw, especially for Max. I heard him pounding on my door, making everything rattle within a close distance to it, and screaming, "You are a fucking dick, Ben. Just know that. You just wait…you'll have yours coming."

I hadn't bothered opening the door because I'd had files and papers sprawled out all over the place, organizing them to hand over to Mr. Richards. I later found out that Max wasn't lying about giving me what I had coming. The ass did put my name on a list. It was the newest one and it was for young citizens with Intranet authorization who believed that the original Constitution should be reinstated. The list was aptly named The Stop Progress List. I must say, if this world was considered progress there was a large part of me that was all for stopping it.

One Friday afternoon Mr. Richards sent a connection over to my apartment with the weekend's list of information that I needed to retrieve. I thanked the guy, who gave me the willies. He was so obvious that it seemed suspicious. He had darkened teeth, and a few were missing, plus snarly hair that was tucked under a stocking cap. He was the type of guy who would have just been called homeless in the days before I was born, but now he was called Socially Unmanageable.

I made myself a quick supper before opening up the envelope to see what awaited me.

"What do you think we'll have going on tonight, Otto?" I ask. Otto answers me with a small paw swat on my leg. "Yah, I don't know either."

Truth be told, the hacking for Mr. Richards is losing some of its luster, and although I'd managed to save half as much as I earned in a year the money does not seem worth it. I didn't like being isolated, and sensed that Mr. Richards enjoyed watching it happen to me.

Today's envelope is rather thick, and I am a bit surprised that it isn't on a drive. I have only gotten a small amount of information on paper thus far. The instructions always contained about three pages of information that was deemed relevant for me, and some key information to aid me in the direction of my hacking endeavors.

The first sheet, which was labeled Priority One, was to find out some information on the employees computer searches at work. Those companies were ones that were very familiar to me: Single Source, MatraTex, and Govern Manage. My heart starts pounding. Amy, Cal, and Max each work for one of those companies. What is going on?

I start to read the other three assignments, labeled Priorities Two, Three, and Four, and I can't read fast enough. When I see the names Amy Fireen, Cal Danville, and Max Gerault I think I am going to lose it. No! How in the hell did their names get on Mr. Richards radar, and more importantly, why are they there? Thoughts of blackmailing came to mind. Sure, he knew who they were because of me, but why did he need all this information on them? I'd kept up my end of the deal.

My mind is in a blur, and I pace around my apartment slamming my fist down on the table occasionally, sending waves of pain surging through it that make me even angrier. Otto is scared and cowering in the corner like the day I'd found him. I realize that I am acting crazy, and stop so I won't scare him. I lean over, trying to pick him up and he runs away until I say I am sorry, and get down on my knees, offering a left-over bite of hamburger from my supper.

My entire body is shaking as I think about my information retrieval tasks for the weekend. What is going on? There is no way that I am going to turn over any information on my best friends. If Mr. Richards wants it so badly he can find some other hacker to get it for him. We are a rare breed, but certainly not impossible to find.

Controlling all the thoughts that are racing through my mind is not easy. So many scenarios and none of them favorable play out. I decide that regardless of what may happen to me I need to do something to alert my friends. Mr. Richards isn't going to get anything from me, and that is the only option.

Chapter Five: July 15, 2042

I charge out of my door with Otto in hand, and make my way to Cal's apartment. I know everyone will be there. I don't bother taking time to knock, and turn the knob and charge in, startling everyone.

"Look who showed up," Max begins sarcastically. "And to what do we owe this honor?"

"Listen. I have to tell you something, and I don't have time to go back and forth about why I haven't been around. This is fucking serious, and it involves you guys."

"What involves us?" Cal asks, standing up.

"Is it safe to talk?" I ask.

"Why wouldn't it be? What's going on?" Cal continues. Amy runs over to the door, and locks it.

"Talk Ben—now." Amy crosses her arms, and I stare at my friends, hoping to find the words that will make sense about something that I do not fully understand.

"Remember when I had to bust into the TerraCorp system for Cal?" Everyone nods yes. "Well, I got busted by one of the upper's there—Mr. Richards."

"Shit. Are you in hot water?" Cal asks. "I'm sorry man."

"Instead of turning me in the guy made a deal with me. He's been paying me a fee to hack on certain companies and individuals. I don't know the exact connection yet, but there is one."

"And you obviously had to keep silent," Amy adds. "Why break the silence now?"

"You three are on my list for this weekend. I don't know why, and I'm not going to turn anything over or hack you, but now I'm not sure what'll happen as a result. I…"

The apartment door is suddenly lying down on the ground, kicked in by a big beast of a man. He is definitely not MCU, and is wearing a different type of uniform. His uniform is a dark green suit, and he is pointing some weapon that I don't recognize. "Stop right there or I'll disintegrate your hands with one shot of this baby. It'd be pretty hard to hack then, wouldn't it?"

We all freeze, unsure of what to do or who this guy is. I realize that I am clinging on to Otto for dear life, and he is barking from the commotion and shaking too. The armed guy's uniform isn't from any branch of Government that I am familiar with, and I don't know what his purpose is. "It's me you want, isn't it?" I ask, hoping to avoid having anything happen to my friends as a result of the situation I am in.

Out of nowhere, Max throws the lamp that is on the table toward the guy, and screams for me to run and get the hell out of there. The lamp hits the guy's hand and he automatically fires the weapon, but it is facing toward the wall. Now there is a hole in the wall that shows the neighbor's living room. He's an older man and he is sitting on his couch, wide eyed, and without an arm.

Before the guy can fire again, one of his back-ups comes in behind him, and Cal charges toward the door, trying to shove him backward. I want to help, and quickly release Otto to grab a chair from the small kitchen table and toss it at them. It lands short, and I suddenly became aware of everyone shouting out that I should run. The uniformed goons are barking orders. "Shut them up, and don't let Danrick run."

I charge off toward Cal's bedroom, calling for Otto to come with me. As soon as he squeaks through the door I slam it shut—an obviously temporary fix. The bedroom is the only window in the apartment, and I go over to it, trying to pry it open. It is stuck shut, and I take the small television that is in the room, and smash it through the window. I put Otto in my backpack, and tried to assess the next part of the plan quickly—there is no time to spare.

Once the window was pried open, I could hear someone at the door, starting to kick at it. I look down from the fourth story that I am on. There is an escape ladder there, and I breathe in, as I make my way out of the window and onto the ladder. I am not a huge fan of heights, and my athletic abilities are definitely subpar. So, this may be simply a fire escape ladder to most people, but to me it is a challenging task. Can I easily rush down this thing with big ass thugs pursuing me, and carrying Otto in my backpack? I'll find out because I don't have any time to create an alternative plan.

I swing onto the ladder and began to scale down it as quickly as my shaking legs can take me. I can feel my heart racing, and I keep looking up, hoping that no one else is getting ready to join me on that ladder, unless it is Max, Cal, or Amy. I make it down three stories, and then stumble, losing my grip as a result. I fall to the pothole filled alleyway and land with a big thud on my belly. Thankfully I did not flip over or else Otto would be crushed. I've lost my breath and am gasping for air, and trying to remain calm. I look up to the open window in Cal's apartment. Otto is whimpering, and the scene is fucking mad…surreal.

The guy who'd shown himself first in Cal's apartment is standing up in the window, pointing his weapon at me. Another dude is talking to someone from his headset. Somehow, I manage to get up and begin running. I dive around the corner and into the adjoining alleyway only to trip over something lying on the ground in the darkness. I look down and see a body, and there is a hole through the entire midriff of it. I can see that it is a guy, but it is not just some random guy—it is the man who delivered me the envelope earlier. Vile starts to fill my throat, and I lean over and purge it out. I don't understand what is going on, and don't know what the hell I am going to do now. I am running from unknown mad men who seem to want to kill me, or capture me and do hell only knows what. The thing that really stinks is that I don't have any money, an ID, or a place to go.

I hear heavy footsteps charging toward my direction, and I take off running as quickly as I can, making my way to a main street. There are still people on the sidewalk, as it isn't curfew yet, and I weave in and out of them. I keep bumping into them, and can hear the people swearing at me, or questioning what is going on. I don't dare call out that I am sorry in case the guys chasing me can possibly hear my voice. For all I know, I have some tracer planted on me that I am not aware of, and they don't have to chase me at all. They will know where I go. Personal invasion is a priority with the Machine, and they don't consider anything off limits for anyone.

Finally, I can't run anymore, and I dive into another alleyway that is pitch black. I hope that I will not find any people there, and I plop in the corner, just behind a bunch of garbage cans. They stink so badly, but I don't dare move. What am I going to do? I'd never had to do anything close to surviving outside without any resources available to me.

I am finally able to take Otto out my backpack, something I couldn't do earlier because he wasn't wearing his tags and collar when I'd taken him over to Cal's. Now, I don't have that or a leash, and I am not about to let any MCU take him away for not being properly documented in public.

Eventually I fall asleep with Otto in my arms, and wake up to the sounds of shuffling feet. People are making their way to work, and starting their days. I remain hidden the best I can all day, growing increasingly starving and thinking about how I am going to handle this situation. I can't stay in this alley forever. I manage to find a few pieces of crust from an old pizza for Otto to eat, but I am not about to go there yet.

All day long two questions weigh on my mind. What do those guys want with me, and my friends? And, are my friends okay?

Chapter Six: July 16, 2042

I find an old baseball hat lying in one of the random alleyway's that I am now roaming down in efforts to stay out of sight now that the sun is up. I place it on my head, and hope that it doesn't have lice in it, or some other nasty thing that may plant itself on my scalp. Still, I have to remain anonymous, and think things through.

The only thing that keeps my mind off of a serious lack of food and hungry belly is replaying through all of the information that I have received. I can only assume that Mr. Richards sent those guys to come get me, and had known that I talked about what I was doing for him to my friends. Other than that, I still didn't know why I was doing the searches for him, and what his intentions were for them. This is so crazy, as well as everything that has happened so quickly the past twenty four hours. It is almost like Richards knew ahead of time that I would go and confess what I'd been up to. Why bother giving me the assignment then?

"Hey, what are you doing out here?" The voice breaks my concentration, and I look up at who asked, trying to remain hidden in the shadows of the hat's bill.

"I'm just making my way back home," I say. It is MCU, and I instantly feel nervous about having to talk to him. I keep staring at his radio and gun.

"Got any ID?"

"Sorry, I was just mugged man, and they took it all."

"Is that your dog?"

"Yah."

"Where's his tags, collar, and leash?"

"The pricks took that too. I guess there's a hot black market for that sort of thing."

"Show your shoulder." The guy pulls out his weapon and holds it closely, and moves in toward me slowly, as if he is ready to pounce on me if I do anything or worse yet—shoot me.

The MCU guy isn't going to let me just be on my way. That much is clear. I really don't want to show my number, and let this guy write it down because it's too risky. Without any real choice, I start to remove my shirt to show my number because I certainly cannot outmuscle or run this guy. My energy is running on low, and my heart is pounding so damn hard. As I start to slowly unbutton my shirt the MCU's communication and command unit goes off, rambling some code to signify an emergency happening somewhere. He looks at me, and says, "Wait right there, and do not move."

"No sir," I say. He turns his back, and I bolt as quickly as I can. Citizen Number 20571289 is safe for the moment. I run onto the main street, and happen to land in front of one of the Public Safety Billboards, and find myself staring directly at me. On the board is a digital image of me with the words, "Dangerous and wanted. Significant reward for live capture."

Live capture is good, but being wanted for being dangerous sucks. I put my head down and continued to walk, hoping that no one will recognize me. They have put those digital billboards up every few blocks in the city. A thought finally occurs to me, one that I wish I would have thought of last night. I need to make my way to find that Felix guy. What is the name of the club he hung out at again? Fray…yah that's it.

I happen to know that Fray is about six blocks from where I am at the moment, and I wonder how I am going to be able to remain safe until I can make my way there when it gets darker. Maybe I can hide nearby, and I'll be able to see Felix when and if he enters the club. He said he was there every night, and that should definitely include tonight. It is Saturday after all, the night where many people like to go out. I just don't happen to be one of them, and I'd give anything to be sitting in my apartment right now and hanging out with Otto in quiet bliss.

This is all so stressful, so unknown. I can't make heads or tails of anything, and know that no answers will come until I know I am safe to think without fear of the Machine swooping down on me, and doing whatever the hell it is they wish to do to me. Damn, my head hurts from all this.

People start to ignore me, thinking I am some vagrant bum. That is standard because they just know that the MCU will come and take care of it. They don't need to worry, and better yet—they don't need to get involved. That's what happens in a micromanagement authoritarian Government. The Government controls everything, and the citizens step aside and don't give a flying fuck about anything other than their self. *Okay, that is not everyone, but it does describe far too many people.*

A loud voice that is vaguely familiar starts coming closer. I peak around the corner on which I am standing at and see Felix there, and he is making his way toward what must be the club entrance with a group of two other people. Although it is getting darker, I can see that they are all tattooed as they stand under a street light, waiting for the perfect time to enter the club. The MCU passes by every fifteen minutes like clockwork, and that is why they are basically ineffective for preventing true tragedies. Everyone who wishes to do no good understands their patterns. Tonight I am one of those people who will benefit from that, but I just want to be safe—not do anything bad.

Five minutes later, Felix makes his way down a set of stairs with a boarded up door. I see him knock on the boards and the door opens up, and he slides in.

Ten minutes later the MCU passes by again, and I quickly dart across the street and go down to the door, and knock. "Yes?"

"I need to speak with Felix."

"I don't know who you are talking about."

"He invited me."

"Name."

"Ben Danrick."

"Come back after the next MCU round, and I'll open the door to see if you can enter."

That was that, and I am back in hiding until the MCU passes by again. So help me, if Felix doesn't give the okay for me to enter I don't know what I'll do. I'd be royally screwed, and might as well go back to my apartment and turn myself in to whoever wants me.

I knock again, and the door instantly opens. A big arm pulls me in aggressively, and another person quickly pats me down. I guess they are making sure I am not armed. It startles me, and irks me. *Even a small guy with a weapon can do some serious harm,* I caution myself. At least I have discovered that Felix really was kidding when he'd mentioned a cavity search that day.

"Well, I knew that I'd be seeing you eventually…not just on the Public Safety Billboards. You've gotten yourself in some serious shit, my scrawny friend."

"I don't even understand it yet, but I'm hoping you can help me out."

"Let's go back into my private quarters and talk about it." Then, as an afterthought he adds, "Oh hey, a dog. Let me hold the little scraggler."

Without hesitation, Felix grabs Otto and Otto was surprisingly mellow about it. I follow Felix and Otto through the maze of rooms. It seems like more of a safe house, or a speak easy that had existed over one hundred thirty years ago. Felix is obviously very popular at Fray, and everyone s treating him like he is the ruler of the underground mad roost. It is fascinating, and I wonder what he does. What is his story aside from being a nice guy with a huge smart ass presence, to warrant such respect and reverence? I can assume he is well connected because nobody aside from hackers really has access to interesting things unless they are.

Once we are back in his private quarters I begin to tell the story of everything that has happened while Otto walks around the room, sniffing everything. Felix listens, and looks at me as if I am saying something commonplace. He is one heck of a tough bastard to figure out, and I suspect that he likes it that way. He is a wild version of the Machine, that's what he was.

"So, do you think you can help me out?"

"I think I may be able to do so, but it won't be easy."

"I don't have access to my money, but you may be able to get into my old apartment and get it."

"It's likely long gone. Plus, this Richards doesn't seem like much of a fuck-up so he probably had that money traced anyways. There's no way I want it traced back to me by any trail—no way man."

"Well, what do you want for payment?" I ask.

"Yet to be determined."

"Should I be scared?"

He ignores my question, choosing to respond differently. "I think you have more abilities and chutzpah than you let on, Ben. At least I'm going to bet on that because you are in one tough situation, and you won't make it out of it alive if you don't have some backbone. You got backbone?"

"I'm getting it...not by choice," I say, knowing that Felix will know I am full of it if I try to say I already have it.

"Good, very good."

"Let's get you some food, and your faithful little sidekick," Felix says abruptly. He excuses himself briefly, and comes back a few minutes later. Fifteen minutes later a sandwich, cold beer, and fries are sitting in front of me. It is so damn good, and I can't even believe the great fortune. Beer is very hard to come by, and although it is not technically illegal it created ridiculous problems if you get busted with it.

The food instantly revives me, and I begin to tell Felix what I need to do first. I need to get into TerraCorp somehow, and find out as much as I can on Mr. Richards. He is the center of this puzzle piece, and once I find out information on him I will be able to formulate a plan, and find out what I was meant to do. I am facing one of those moments that people often refer to as their moment of truth. I need to discover how me, a person of no real means, can survive and come out of this situation on top. I need to do that, especially for my friends who put themselves in great danger to help me escape.

Chapter Seven: July 20, 2042
It's hard to imagine that it is me looking in this mirror. I look clean cut, official, and like I am not capable of smiling. *That part might be true right now.* All of this is for the purpose of disguising my looks as I make my way toward TerraCorp to investigate. If I don't find any leads I am fully aware of just how screwed I am too.

Felix has somehow come up with a fake identification for me with clearance codes to all levels of TerraCorp. He is resourceful, almost too resourceful, but I don't have a choice. He hasn't steered me wrong yet, and I don't believe he will. And even if I suspected it, I don't really have a choice right now.

Otto is looking at me with a tilted head, no doubt thinking that his owner's gone crazy. My dyed blonde hair is cut short, hiding the dark curls that I'd have naturally and making me look like I could be Swedish or something like that. I'm not sure if that is really a positive thing because ever since the US hacked into their computers, trying to siphon money out of their national treasury we've been on shaky terms. The old history books show that we feared the Middle East, but I guess that you ultimately end up fearing everyone that you piss off eventually. Nope, Sweden isn't quite as relaxed a government as most people had imagined before the Machine started to rumble.

I can feel the sweat on my palms as I sneak in the shadows, making my way to a back entrance of TerraCorp. All of the regulars have gone home for the day, and I really don't know if they'd recognize me. I'm definitely not taking a chance. The back entrance is barely used by anyone since it is meant for deliveries, and for higher ups to sneak in unexpectedly.

The card easily passes through the swipe, and I am impressed. Next is the eye scan, and I'm nervous. I have in some irritating contacts that Felix gave me, and when I put them in they felt like they melted right to my eyeballs. I breathe in, and stand still, allowing the blue laser beam to scan my eyes, and call out, "Retinal and DNA match confirmed. Entrance granted. Enter code."

The machine talks like a woman with no sense of humor, like one of the disciplinarians in the girls' juvie homes that run abundantly across the country, filled to capacity with young girls who dared speak their mind or challenge the Machine.

I'm a bit freaked at how long the process is taking. Is something wrong? I listen, and don't hear any noise other than my heart. It's pounding in my head like a tympani drum, making it hard to focus. Finally, I hear the sentence that I want, and punch in the code that I hacked at Felix's place from the security office of TerraCorp. I'm in.

I sneak up to the second floor, dodging under cubicles as I hear people approaching. There are not many, but some of them are the higher ups, and others in charge of cleaning the office. I make my way into the riskiest office in the building for me—Mr. Richards. I saw him leave earlier, as he always does on this day, and that's how I know that today is the day. There is no other option.

His office is solid walls on the front side, and all glass on the back. It's pretty damn righteous, and the type of place that I could see hacking in. The actual sunlight would be inspirational, but the Machine, and corporate higher ups guard it like it was just meant for them. I think the pricks are afraid that it'll inspire someone to break free from their own personal hell. That's one thing that I've thought about and daydreamed about since I was a young kid. Of course, it's easy to forget those dreams because the sun doesn't shine like it used to.

Sitting down in the chair of Mr. Richards is an odd feeling. It's softer and plusher than anything my skinny ass has ever sat on. Love it. Want it. *Focus. You probably have less than twenty minutes to get in, and get out.*

As I start typing I immediately notice that there is a sticky substance on the keyboard. Tricky bastards put an adhesive on there to snatch prints of anyone who may try to use it. It doesn't matter now because there's no turning back, and I start diving in layer after layer until I reach the deepest levels of TerraCorp, as well as Mr. Richards personal computer accounts. Why would he send emails from TerraCorp to his personal account? He seems smarter than that. It doesn't make any sense.

One file captures my interest as I look through all the off kilter searches on Richards TerraCorp computer, and home computer. It's a folder titled, "CN Search". The only CN that we all seem to relate to is Citizen Number. Anyone who is interested in that number aside from the Machine is definitely up to something…most likely related to corruption.

Each number in the file is indeed a CN, as identified by seeing mine in the list. I begin to quickly open up the files, perusing the information on each one of them as quickly as possible. My eyes scan the pages fast, and I memorize them with laser speed accuracy, absorbing every detail and then moving on to the next one. I see my friends' names in there, a few unknown names, and the names of the people that I'd searched on. I quickly go to the next file, marked BN, likely for Business Number, and find some of the businesses I dug up dirt on, and a few that were likely ones that I would have been doing in the near future. I move faster and faster, sweating until I'm soaked as I try to memorize all the information as quickly as possible.

This is insane, and all of these people are connected in some way. I have parts of the puzzle solved, but not the entire thing. It's crazy, and something about these people obviously threatens Mr. Richards. *Or does it benefit him?*

I wipe my forehead, trying to keep the sweat out of my eyes. I'm so hot, and I almost feel like I could puke. My adrenaline is surging through me, and my eyes are getting blurry. Damn it. I have to focus. There's no way I can pass out here…no fucking way or I'll be dead. There won't be any mercy on me after doing this. Richards will turn me over to the ITC, or have one of his goons off me in the alley, like they did that one bum who delivered me the files that started all this spiraling out of control.

A loud thud sounds on the door, which is thankfully locked, and I freeze. Suddenly I hear a few thuds coming, and I sense that they are the butt end of guns. I jump up, and quickly log out of the entire system as I'm doing so. The door finally smashes open, and I see the familiar face of the guy who busted down Cal's door staring at me.

I am trapped between these guys, and a glass window. Should I jump? Could I even break that glass? You'd think it would be bullet proof. I'm so panicked. *Think. Think.* I see a bronze vase in the corner of the office and reach over to grab it. The entire time the guys are pointing their guns at me, daring me to charge past them. I don't think so…that is not going to happen. They don't expect me to toss the vase with all the might I have through the glass window, but I do it. Glass goes flying everywhere, instantly making small painful slits on my arms, and face. The sweat stings them instantly, and I can feel pain zipping through my body. Without a second thought, I grab the keyboard and jump out the window, not knowing what is below me.

I land on prickly decorative bush in a clay planter's box, and it smashes to the ground from my weight as I slam into it. I find myself not being able to breathe very easily, and equally surprised that I've fallen to the earth from the sky for the second time in a week. There's a guy pointing a hand gun at me from up above. I try to roll, and avoid it, but it's almost like my hearing is ultra sensitive. I swear I can hear the release of the trigger and the sound of the bullet flying down at me. It hits my leg.

Blood splatters up into my face, and I instinctually grab my leg, hoping it will make the searing pain go away. I've never felt anything like it, and it's miserable. Absolutely miserable. There's a woman screaming from across the street, drawing attention when I don't want any more. I jump up, hobbling away as fast as I can.

* * *

"Well done. Did you get him?"

"Yes sir, Mr. Richards. In the leg."

"Excellent. That's just enough to scare him."

Mr. Richards looks over to his desk, and adds, "Smart move taking the keyboard. I may have underestimated Ben Danrick a bit."

Chapter Eight: July 20, 2042

I cannot stop shaking, and I hope I make it back to the Fray before anyone catches me. There seems to be more MCU out tonight, and I can't tell if I'm paranoid or if they are after me. I've got to stay calm and focus so I don't get my ass busted, and I have to remember everything I saw tonight. I can't believe I had to jump out a second story window. That is balls out crazy. I really didn't have a choice though and I am so curious about what Mr. Richard is thinking. He obviously knows I busted into his office by now, and he's probably set to unleash his wrath on me, just like he did at Cal's apartment.

Everything suddenly starts spinning around me, and everything around me becomes blurry, like I'm looking through fog. Voices are talking to me, and fading in and out like they are trying to mess with my mind, or I am on some sort of trip. Crap. I'm falling.

I don't know how long I have been out for, but I open my eyes to find me slung over the shoulder of a big guy that I don't know. I recognize the area—it's by the Fray—but the entrance that the guy is taking me into isn't the one I've used in the past. I suddenly hear Felix's voice, and I can tell he is rushing around, shouting out orders to everyone. They are all moving quickly. Fuck…are Richards men here to get me?

"What's going on?" I ask, barely able to get my words out.

"Keep quiet. You're seriously messed up, and need to save whatever energy you got left," Felix snaps. He does not sound lighthearted, cynical, or composed like he usually does. He is seriously freaked out…and badly at that.

I am placed on a cot in a small room that doesn't contain much else. I still can't focus, and am struggling to keep my eyes open. The walls are made of cement, and I can see the moisture from the ground making them glisten. It is some sort of cellar, and I don't recognize it. "What is this place?"

"It's the safe room."

"Why am I here, and not where I've been sleeping?"

"You are out of commission, man. That's why you're here. If anyone should surprise us they'd never find you here."

"Oh." I think I fall asleep. I wake up again, not sure of how long I've been out. There is a young woman in the corner sitting in a chair, and reading a magazine. I stare at her, my mouth too dry to talk. Even though I'm in pain and half delirious I can tell that she is rather beautiful with her raven black hair and bright green eyes. She finally notices me staring.

"Ah, you're awake then. How are 'ya doing?" Her voice had a thick accent, one that I don't recognize.

"Thirsty."

"I suppose. I'll go get you some water, and be back in a spiff."

She is true to her word, and comes back a few minutes later with water, and Felix.

"I'm glad you're awake. You're a fucking maniac, you know that. Jumping out of a mother fucking window…fucking insane."

I smile, wondering how many more times he could sling an f-bomb out there in one statement. "I just may be fucking insane, Felix." I whisper before pausing to take a long drink of water. I begin to cough, sending the water trickling down my chin and spraying about the bed.

"Careful there. Take it slow," the woman says.

"What's your name?" I croak.

"Gia. I'm going to help you heal your busted body so you can get on to bigger and better things then. Sound good?"

"I'm in some serious pain."

"You're morphed up to the maximum right now. Any more and you'll be nuttier than squirrel shit." Felix chuckles at his joke, and I smile. I am already exhausted and ready to sleep again.

I know that Felix is making some general conversation, but it is hard to focus on it. My mind, fuzzy as it is, keeps wandering to thoughts of Cal, Amy, and Max. I think I am talking and asking Felix if he can find out if my friends are okay for me. I think he nods yes, but I can't be sure. Sleep is overtaking me. Deep down I know that it is giving me a temporary reprieve from the throbbing pain running through my entire body and especially my thigh in the place where the bullet has pierced into it.

Once again I wake up, and see Gia sitting in the corner. She is asleep this time though. Otto is nestled in at the foot of the bed, but alert and staring at me. I smile at him, and pat my leg. It's the leg that was shot, and I grimace from the feeling it leaves. Otto comes up to the other side of me, walking carefully across the bed, and licks my cheek. I pet him, and then I look to my right and notice a small tray of food near me. It is cheese, crackers, and sausage, plus a glass of water. I lean over to reach for the water again, sensing that my mouth is so dry that it could possibly crack if I tried to talk.

This time I drink the water more slowly, not wanting to have the same repeat from earlier…whenever earlier was. There is no clock in here, and I have no clue if it is day or night, or even the same day at all. I try reaching for the plate of food next, and end up toppling over a fork that had been placed on the tray. Gia jumps, popping her eyes open immediately. "Nice to see 'ya awake, Ben. How 'ya feeling?"

"Hungry, in pain, and completely disoriented. How's that for a combination?"

"Sucky, I'd say."

"How long did I sleep for?"

"A few days. It's Thursday, right around the noon hour." Gia looks at her watch and shrugs her shoulders.

"Thursday. It was Tuesday night that I went to TerraCorp, right?"

"That's right sport. Been out a good long time. Probably a good thing because you are seriously morphed up and likely in some big time pain. The shock of it all likely made you sleep like that. I must say though, it was entertaining."

"Entertaining?" I ask, not liking the sound of that.

"Let's just say, 'ya talk in your sleep aplenty. Pretty interesting stuff too."

I groan. *Shit, I hope I didn't say too much. My sleep talking is said to be a bit too honest.* Gia lets me off the hook and tells me that it only had to do with hacking stuff, and my friends.

"I think I asked Felix if he could find out how Max, Cal, and Amy were. It's hard to say for sure, but do you happen to know if I did?"

"Not a clue, but I know Felix is eager to chat with you. I'll go get him. Want anything else to eat?"

"Nah, not right now."

Once again, Felix shows himself to me. This time he tells Gia to take a break while he talks to me. There is something he needs to tell me in confidence. My stomach jumps, fearing what it might be. I am probably Public Nuisance Number One now, and if I thought my face was plastered on too many PSBs before, it has probably multiplied.

"Do you remember asking me to find out about your friends, Ben?"

"I thought I did, but wasn't sure. I know I'd meant to and from what you just said I must have."

"Yes or no would have been fine. Save your words and energy for the tasks that lay ahead of you, my friend."

"So, what's the scoop?" I ask, agreeing that it's good to get right to the point.

"I'll be honest and right to the point. There's no easy way to put shit like this. Your friends Max and Amy were killed at that apartment that night."

"And Cal?" I ask, not able to process the thought.

"Word has it that he's been taken, and is in ITC custody. They know that he knows a ton of shit about the Machine, and they plan on using his skills to find ways to make their systems hacker proof."

"And he agreed to that?"

"Yah, I suppose so. If the choice is between a fricking laser beam to the head and cooperation most people will choose cooperation."

"That would be Cal. If you think I'm lacking brawn, you'd think even more so of him."

"All you hackers so scrawny?"

"No, I don't think so. Never tried to network with too many though. You never know who you can trust, you know."

"Isn't that the truth. I know that I've aligned myself with an army of beasty dudes who aren't hesitant to unleash the fury or pound in a Machine lover's head without provocation." Felix smiles, reflecting on his statement as if it was perfectly normal and commonplace.

"You know, I've always hoped that I could have the gift to inspire people through my words if given the opportunity. The muscle has never really factored into my equation."

"We're all given different gifts, Ben. Some of us are designed to be the enforcers, and others are designed to be the motivators. It's cool that you want to motivate, but here's a little advice. That moment of hesitation when you are debating what to do could be all it takes for some ass-munch to blow your head off. It does seem like you just went for it when you jumped out of that window like a wild man, and didn't really toss around the negotiating deal."

"I hesitated, but they were surprised that I did that I think."

"Pretty good assumption, I'd guess."

We are quiet for a moment, and then Felix sighs deeply before talking again. "Look, I can see that you're trying to keep talking about any shit that comes into your mind in order to avoid processing what I told you about your friends. I'm sorry about it, especially the two that died, but I am going to leave you in peace right now. You need to process what happened with them, grieve however you must, and then get over it quickly. What you have to do in the future is no small task, but it does require you to have your shit together."

"You know what I have to do?"

"Just like you do. I just happen to have the means to get you off on the right start. Or at minimum, guarantee you don't jump out of any more windows, get shot, or get busted by the MCU."

"Okay."

"We'll talk tomorrow, Ben. You should be able to move around by then."

"Hey, one more question, Felix." Felix looks at me curiously. "Who took the bullet out of my leg?"

"Gia, she's a rockin' incredible woman, isn't she?"

I smile, not wanting to seem too eager to agree. Even in my dazed state it is hard to not notice that Gia is a good looking woman—the type that I might dream about but probably will never get a chance with. "Well, I'll see you when I can walk to you then."

Felix opens the door to leave. Gia comes back five minutes later, looking plenty pissed about how she finds me. I've gotten up and am trying to walk alongside the bed, holding the mattress for support. "Are you a crazy bloke? You could bust your skull open. Is that what you want then?"

"No, I don't want that. I want to walk so I can walk out of this safe room and out there," I say, pointing toward the door. "I'm going to find Felix, and find out what needs to be done so I can get that prick bastard Richards, who is personally responsible for the death of two of my best friends."

"Anger can motivate, but it can also make you be a dumb-ass prick. Right now I'm seeing the prick, and I suggest you sit your ass down before you bust your head on the concrete walls of this cozy little room. Got it then?"

I look admittedly shocked at how a fairly petite woman can rattle of a rant like that without even getting winded. She is way more intense than me...or at least the me I knew up until a few months ago. *I bet if I said that out loud she'd smack me across the head. It kind of sucks seeing a woman tougher than me. Better work on the machismo...for survival if anything.*

As I doze back off into sleep, exhausted from the half assed attempt to walk I break out into a series of vivid dreams that made me agonize. I keep seeing my friends, and it isn't during the joyful times either. It is their expressions when they are so irate at me for changing so quickly. It is another reason for me to avenge Mr. Richards and make him pay for what he's done. I will do whatever it takes. I am also fully aware that it will take more than words to satisfy my desire for revenge in the name of my friends, and those like us that oppose the Machine. I wake up, realizing that I can see my destiny more clearly in my dreams than I can in my conscious mind.

Chapter Nine: July 24, 2042

It's crazy how something like walking can give you such a rush, but that is what I'm experiencing right now as I make my way toward Felix. I'll admit, it still hurts and I wouldn't be one bit surprised if I collapsed from holding my breath. My cracked ribs that came with the fall are still challenging, but I can do this. Really, there isn't a choice so dwelling on it would be an absolute waste of time, and wankerdom to the extreme.

I make my way to Felix's office, aware that Gia is a few steps behind me. She doesn't realize I know she's there and I don't let on. What's the point? Besides if I do wipe out it is entirely possible that I really may need some help. She's gotten the hang of it because in my determination to walk, regardless of the discomfort and pain, I have tumbled a few times. She has helped each and every time, mumbling about what a shit I am. I'm pretty thankful for her though and when I try to tell her that she just smiles, and calls me a stubborn shit again. I must say, she probably did a better job of helping me out with removing the bullet and everything else than one of the Machine's doctors would have. Knowing the committees that determine care, they might have said *to hell with my leg, I work on a computer anyway.* They are heartless asses that way, rationing care to everyone that isn't a part of the Machine's ass kissing groupies.

Felix's door is closed, and I knock loudly. Thankfully no one can see the wince on my face. Not only is the door metal, but my knuckles are still slightly bruised from smashing into the pavement below me when I lunged out of the window, making it clearly evident that I have no amazing powers of any sort. No bounce…just thud. But that's the past, and it'll never be the same again. Hell, it won't even be similar. If I survive this crap there is an amazingly high chance that I'll be living in refuge for the remainder of my days…or until someone turns over this authoritarian Machine that has basically made life suck for a majority of people. Until now, I never realized that I had so much bitterness festering inside of me. It's time to unleash that…it's time.

I must have spaced out slightly because I am taking note that Felix's door is open, and he is staring at me like I've lost my marbles. "Okay, maybe I wasn't clear enough, Ben. I assumed that when you could walk here you'd also be able to talk."

"Sorry, I just went into a crazy thought induced by my new ultra low dose morph injection."

"It's a good thing you're getting weaned off it too. That shit is addictive, and you've about cleaned out our entire stash with your injury."

"A lot of people need it?"

"More than what you'd ever imagine. It'd make your hacking head spin if you knew."

"Well, I'm going to invite myself in and sit down now, Felix." I turn to Gia and wave that she can go. The only good thing about my pathetic physical condition right now is her company. She cracks me up until I get tears in my eyes…from the broken ribs.

"So, I know what you should do, and you say you know what you should do. Who should go first? It'd really suck if we weren't on the same page, huh?" Felix leans back and props his hands on his head, smiling smugly at me. I notice that his front tooth has a chip in it, and I'm pretty sure it wasn't ever there before. Now's not the time to ask though.

"Well, I'm going to figure out what Richards is up to. I'll do that by piecing together all the clues that I have locked up here," I say, pointing to my head. "And when I do, he's going to pay for what he did, and one more problem in this messed up world will be solved."

"Interesting concept. So you'll feel content, and ready to live life again after Richards is figured out, and erased from existence. What then?"

"I don't really know. I've just assumed that I'll probably be a refuge for the rest of my living days if I survive."

"You are built for more. Why cast your revenge on Richards when he is a guy who is easily replaced by the next greedy bastard that wants to be all important to the Machine?" Felix pauses, and I don't respond; mostly because I have no good answer for that. He takes it as his permission to continue, not that he needs it.

"Ben, remember who I said inspired me on that first day we met?"

"Yah, Dr. Jay Secton."

"Exactly. Most guys don't even have enough testosterone to acknowledge the great Dr. Secton when I bring them up, but you knew who he was and didn't hide it. I have a hunch you could recite that Wall Street Op-Ed from back in 2020 even in a morphed up state. Am I right?"

I nod yes. I do know that entire op-ed by heart, and it is one of the few things that I take utter joy in, and receive inspiration from that is not hacking related. The op-ed has been long banned and removed from the old internet days; however like always, the Machine really doesn't know how to do anything as good as they think they can do. The result is that some of the best hackers are able to get black market copies of the op-ed, even on the new Intranet, and now they have been passing it down for a generation or two, all dependent on one's given age.

"Recite it." I look at Felix, thinking he is being an ass asking me to do that when there are so many important things to discuss. I start reciting it, and when I get to the words *Rogue Spartan* he shouts out for me to stop. It startles me and my leg jumps out, smashing into the front edge of his desk. "Fuck…mellow out, Felix. Damn, that hurt."

Felix laughs, ignoring my obvious pain. "Why did you have me stop there? Convinced that I really know it?"

"The last two words that you said are the important words, Ben."

"Rogue Spartan? It's more like a cult concept than an actual reality for anyone, considering we don't have guns that disintegrate you like the Machine has developed, or resources to do whatever the hell we want in the civilian world."

"Don't be dumb. Why can't you, hacker genius boy, rise above the ashes like a mythical Phoenix, and be the one that turns the Machine on its side, and blasts the fucking crap out of it?"

"Look at me. Do I look like I can handle something like that?"

"Well frankly, no. However, you have me, and I have the resources and means to set you up to do whatever needs to be done, including supporting personnel."

"Are you serious? You think I can be the *Rogue Spartan*?"

"Do I look like I'd say it if I didn't believe it? Stop wasting words, and delaying the inevitable. Do you, or do you not, have the conviction and intelligence to rally people with those words you claim to want to use to motivate, and do whatever the hell it takes to stop the Machine?"

I pause, not sure what to say. Talk of doing the things mentioned in Secton's op-ed and daydreams about them have always been present in my mind. They have been shared with my friends for some laughs, and grandiose notions. They are not thoughts based on reality or true potential, or any expectation them really happening or being possible. Yet, here Felix is, serious as an executioner, telling me that I am to be the one that Dr. Jay Secton talked about over twenty years ago. Could I do it? I am not a forward or aggressive person, but do I have to be those things in order to lead a concept that's as huge as the one that I've loved for so long? I was ten when I read that op-ed for the very first time, actually the only time because I memorized it that day.

"Okay, we've been sitting here in silence for nearly five minutes. My time is valuable. Either you think you can do this thing, or you don't. No pressure, but I want to know in one minute or I'm going to blow your indecisive head off." I look up at Felix, and freeze. The son of a bitch is pointing a small laser gun at me. I don't know what the model is, but I know enough about it to understand that its impact would make my other injuries immediately become irrelevant.

"Damn, Felix, stop it. Put that thing down. Fine, I'll do it, but I will need your help. I don't have a clue how to survive living off the grid while reaching out to people while doing so."

"I can help you there, and I'm glad to hear you came to the right decision, Ben. Otherwise I would have had to kill you, and that would have been a shame. I really like you."

"Thanks," I say, not bothering to hide the sarcasm.

"Consider that your first lesson in quick decision making and mental toughness."

I couldn't help but notice the word first. What was I in store for?

"Your first assignment is finding a place where we can go. The criteria are that it is off the grid, access to technology, and room for you and your small team to live comfortably, and take care of the task at hand."

"Where can I go to research that? And who is on this team?"

"The team is Gia, and three other associates of mine— tough ass bastards to protect you from threats, and protect me from you if you become one. As for research, I'll take you to where you can have all the privacy, technology and access you need. Right now, I need you to go and get your scrawny ass back to sleep. You are going to need all the energy you can get for tomorrow."

"You don't really need to keep stressing that I have a scrawny ass, Felix. I am well aware without your mention."

"Oh, I'm sorry. I didn't realize that you felt that way. I'll just start calling you Rogue Spartan and spread the word to the millions of people that you are going to be delivering a message of hope to them in your sensitive and motivating style. Sound better?"

I don't bother answering, knowing that Felix could keep going all day long if I let him. It is a better choice to leave his office, and that's what I do. As I walk back to the safe room with Gia following behind me I am half in shock about what I have just signed on to do. What would Max and Amy say if they were alive? Then a thought occurs to me...if I pull this crazy stunt off I might be able to free Cal, and at least I'd still have one of my long time friends back with me.

Chapter Ten: July 27, 2042

There is one saving grace to helping me find a place to take on the task that I've been presented. It still seems surreal to me, and not a destiny that I ever would have envisioned for myself. Some people are meant to change the world and others are meant to get by with what they've been dealt. That's always what I assumed my role was, but now I am looking at being the person to inspire a movement to overthrow a government—correction, the Machine. I need to start being the mad revolutionary who inspires people to be passionate and adopt a do or die attitude.

I pull the diamond stud earring out of my ear, and put it into a reading device, which Felix's lab just happens to have. The guy really is well connected, which makes it more confusing that he would choose me or even choose to help me. Yah, I am great with a computer, but no other quality of Secton's *Rogue Spartan* really applies to me.

Cal's findings over the years are the ones that I really want to focus on and then if I came up with nothing I'd look through Amy's next. The two of them are and were obsessed with everything related to the Machine, and its big agenda. It has all led to a generation of people being born that are just like me—we have never even known what true freedom is or lived in times where the principles that the Constitution were founded on still exist. I've only known the authoritarian government my entire life and it is through obtaining banned and forbidden writings that I have learned what it was ever like back when it was a genuine power and a beacon of hope. I am a product of the propaganda machine, but something has made me not be a blind subscriber like so many others. Granted, I am a good actor because I live in fear of being in the spotlight.

I don't know how long I am looking through all the content, but it is taking a long time to do it. I keep reflecting on the various things that have happened with my friends when we were finding out all the information I am now looking through and I miss them. Truthfully, I am seething deep down and fucking pissed off that they are now taken away from me.

Eventually I go to a file named *Kansas Scapenet*, and open it up. It isn't time to celebrate too early, but I think I may have hit the jack pot with this one. The entire folder of why the government keeps this property maintained for a safe house bunker to this very day is there; along with a schedule and reasons. Why would Cal have ever wanted this? I don't know, but I quickly read the content, printing it off and going to find Felix.

Felix is shooting pool with some of his friends, and waves me over when he sees me. I don't want to waste any time. "You got some time? I think I found something."

"Give me five minutes so I can finish kicking Skullker's ass."

The guy, presumably Skullker, snorts. "One good game, and suddenly a bunch of shit is spewing out of your mouth."

"This is the start of a winning streak that'll last a lifetime. You best get used to it."

I try to remain calm, but don't feel like listening to the banter between these guys as they drink beer and shoot pool. I have found something and I am eager to see if it will fit the criteria. I have already started formulating the reasons that I believe it will, but I know that even though I am the one designated to bringing down the Machine I still need Felix and his resources…at least until I learn a bit more about actual survival off the grid. Hacking off the grid easy—survival questionable.

"You look impatient. I'm going to guess that's good."

"I think it might be."

"Let's go to the office," Felix says. He turns to Skullker and tells him to find Gia, and send her in too.

The second we are in the office and the door is closed I tell Felix that I've found a great location that should work for our purposes.

"Where is that?"

"Salina, Kansas."

"You're kidding. Isn't that place known for tornadoes and shit."

"Not this bunker's location. Proven safe through all of time and nestled in the foothills of the Smoky Mountains. Furthermore, it's only accessible entrance is on the side of the Great Plains and you can see things for miles from its location. No one occupies it, it's kept fully prepared for the elite of the Machine in case of an unanswered attack via either cyber warfare or traditional warfare. This place covers it all and is as high tech as the Pentagon used to be before the Machine let it crumble down into shambles."

"And no one occupies it?"

"They do yearly maintenance, which it seems was just completed this past month. It's been that way for the past fifteen years, and has always fallen within a few weeks of the date. No reason to believe it was different this year."

"But you don't have that information to confirm?"

"No, but this is the place. It's centrally located in the States, pretty safe, isolated, and has options. We are not going to find any better."

Felix looks at me, smiling casually. "Well, you sound determined. I'll send a party out, and if it looks good to go we will have you and the team delivered there within a week."

"Excellent."

"Any idea on how you'll scramble signals and find alarms that alert the Machine someone is there?"

"That is one thing I can definitely take care of thanks to Cal and Amy. Those two provided me with answers without even knowing that I'd ever need them. It was there little thing they got off on, invading the Machine. Now it may be just the thing that allows me to avenge their death and the MCU who did it. Those bastards will pay, and I don't care how you think about me wanting revenge because I do and nothing will change that."

"No need to keep repeating it. I believe you, Ben."

"Do you need anything else? I have work to do, and plans to make."

"Oh yah, just one more thing. From now on, Ben Danrick is wiped off the face of the earth for all practical purposes, and *Rogue Spartan* is on the rise."

"Wiped out? What do you mean by that?"

"If you tried to hack yourself you'd be at a dead end. How's that for anonymity?"

"I'm not sure, but what does it really matter. The day I turned on Richards everything changed."

Chapter Eleven: September 18, 2042

Life in the bunker is routine to say the least. Gia is helpful with piecing together all the information I am busy accessing, but also a bit distracting. I need this information to make sense of what the Machine is up to so I can stop them, but every time she speaks to me her accent gets to me, managing to arouse certain parts of me—parts that it is not easy to hide for me, a guy who is not a smooth talker or used to being in close proximity to a woman like Gia for extended periods of time.

After finding out what Richards is up to I need to motivate the forces, namely citizens who oppose the Machine and are waiting for the right time to lash out. It is not a small task or one to be taken lightly; however, the Machine's arrogance has failed to factor in how big this group is and I am hoping that they will see that I can take them the distance. I have actually started believing it a bit myself. Each day brings a bit more confidence in the madness that I am someone who has the power to change big things.

The bunker itself is rather large, covering about five thousand square feet. Otto has settled right in and is the ruler of the roost. Everyone likes him and he is pretty good with everyone else too. It is strange and I have never seen him so relaxed since I took him home five years ago. In the bunker there are enough small bedroom apartments for each of us to have our own, a kitchen, an exercise area, a lounge, and then a computer lab that is unlike anything that I have ever thought was created yet, plus some smaller storage areas for food and other supplies. I think the bunker seems almost too good to be true because it appears to have been built just for me and the mission I am taking on. If it would have been logical, you would have thought they wanted someone to actually oppose the Machine. Plus, it couldn't be the only bunker in existence and why would you need multiples?

My security detail is all muscle and consists of three of the biggest guys I have ever seen. Fox, Traps, and Pounder make the MCU look like tea cup poodles—they are that big of dogs. I can't lie about their presence making me feel safe though. Also, they do not take the task of trying to get me into a bit better shape lightly. I want to be fit enough to run my ass of if I need to escape someone or at least deliver them a good blow before fleeing. They tell me that improving my physical health will do more for me mentally than I have probably imagined too. That is a theory that has existed for a long time and it has also been applied by many people over the past century. I have just never taken the time to investigate it, or had the desire. Just four months ago I was the guy who sat waiting for my bus trying to look invisible. Big guys are not invisible because they instill instant fear into scrawny guys like me. That is something that had always been true over time too. I finally admit they are right though and when I am really stuck or my brain is really fried from staring at computer screens the work-out often helps me. I can even do 100 push-ups in a row now, a 200% improvement from the time I arrived at the bunker.

One day while Gia and I are laying out all of the pieces of information that we have found and connecting the ones that make sense to us we finally begin to think we may have made some progress. It gives me hope that I am close to finding a way to figure out Richards' angle. We have everything laid out on a logic board and have come to few conclusions based off of the information, and they can be confirmed by information I have been able to hack. The most important conclusion is that Richards seemed to have it in for corrupting the higher ups for the Machine. He is well positioned within it, but doesn't have the same luxuries and securities as many of the higher ups. He obviously is ambitious, and he had done well by bringing down a great many people; including the President's brother who had been the MCU Grand Chief, company heads, and various other people serving on the different boards of President Redman. It is a big concern that Virilian Industries and LaserMachination are now government controlled completely. That has happened within the past month. The two companies provide a sure means to eliminate people with either an air contagion or disintegrate them with a potent laser. There are even experiments being conducted that will combine the two together, and allow the Machine the ability to deliver contagions to people through their Intranet networks, maybe through medical equipment, and through the guns that the MCU carries around on their patrols.

Gia is looking at everything closely, tapping her chin with her pointer finger. "Something doesn't add up all right. I get Redman wanting to secure his position, that's his deal. He's an egomaniac wanker after all. What I don't get is the connection between Redman and Richards. Do you think that Redman has hired Richards to help him?"

"Maybe. Why would Redman want so many of his higher ups eliminated though? They couldn't all have turned on him, could they?"

"Nope. Doesn't make much sense, yet it seems quite logical. I can't prove it right or wrong, but there is a possibility that Redman is setting up these higher ups to jockey his way up the ladder of the Machine. He's seems to embrace the pathological tendencies of those sorts. Anyone with the moxie to stand up to him or get in his way of what he thinks of as progress is wiped out by setting them up."

"That sounds overly complicated."

"To us it does, Ben. To him, it's really that simple. You're the only one who knows him. Is that the impression you got?"

"Not completely, but I'm not really known for being a great judge of character; especially when I'm being blackmailed for hacking."

"Good point. That shows that he's willing to use people though, and that's a start," Gia said. "I'm guessing the main question for you is what Richards is up to. We get the general idea of his actions. Do you think that is important to get started with the rest of the plan then, Ben?"

I look at Gia. I know what she is hinting at. Revenge on Richards is my little joy, but it is not what Felix and company has signed on for. They want full out rebellion and the creation of a militia that doesn't fear the Machine. They are willing to sacrifice anything and everything to make it stop. Of course, they only really have their lives left to give. Everything else, aside from family, has no real value any longer. There are not even deeds and titles to show ownership to anything, and a centrally run bank is the only option for putting your money into. Most people choose the risk of theft at their home compared to having the Machine steal their money from the bank if it feels like it, or is out to get the person for something they perceive to be wrong.

"Gia, I do know that it is time to start bringing the *Rogue Spartan* to the people, and seeing what happens. I've never delivered powerful words to the masses before, and I am a bit nervous about my words really motivating people. It sounded better saying it back then than it sounds now. I was just talking out of my ass."

"Don't be a shit and keep discrediting yourself. It's annoying, and unbecoming to those of us who believe in you already."

Damn, she has such a sting in her words when she is pissed. "I'll work on it, and we'll deliver my first stage of that plan within two weeks time."

"And what is that first stage then? Can you tell me yet, and when you going to get off your arse and clear it through Felix?"

"Yah I know. For some reason he trusts me, but not that much," I comment. Who can blame him though? I have no proven record of doing anything bold and he lives a bold life. It's been that way from the time he was born and continues on.

"Exactly," Gia says. This time she smiles at me, which is certainly much more preferable. Felix should have her running the show. She is fearless and doesn't take any shit. "So, what is the plan?"

"I'll discuss it with Felix first." I start to laugh because Gia does an uncharacteristically childish thing and sticks her tongue out at me. Withholding information is her weakness…at least she has one that I can identify.

So, per the not so subtle suggestion from Gia, I put my revenge on Richards on hold, knowing that the time will eventually come. Instead, I focus on how I am going to deliver a message that inspires people who may lose their lives or be imprisoned for the remainder of them to help me bring down the Machine, and restore the original constitution of the land. *No pressure.*

Chapter Twelve: October 1, 2042
Everything is set for the broadcast, starting with Felix's delight of the idea. He loves it, and says that it is rebel righteous. I'm not sure if that's what I'd call it, but I have grown used to his unique terminology the past months. He has even come down to the bunker to watch me broadcast live. I am nervous enough and can't help wondering if he is going to be able to remain quiet while I do my thing. I write down some notes and a general outline, but don't write my broadcast out in full. Gia tells me that I will not be able to inspire one of my enemies, such as the MCU, to come and get me if I just read the script. Apparently I need passion and the type of conviction that only comes from speaking from the heart. My heart mourns the loss of my friends and that is going to be the fuel to my fire. As for the passion…I am thinking Gia may provide that even if she doesn't know it.

In order to prepare for the broadcast we are going extreme. We are prepared to hijack some radio waves from the Machine and are going to cut into the FABS (Federally Approved Broadcasting System) to deliver the message. Time is critical and I am hoping for at least five minutes before we are cut off. Then it will be time to lay low and not communicate in any way whatsoever. I will be isolated, as well as the rest of the team, and we will all have to live wondering what is going on. The orders are to not do anything else until Felix delivers word that it is safe to do so.

Felix is pacing around, looking more nervous and edgy than me minutes before it is time for action.

"You're sure everything is in place, and functional?"

"Yes."

"Remember RS, we cannot afford to have any failures here or we'll have lost months of preparation time, and I'll be so pissed that you don't know what I'll do." *Half the time I don't even realize I'm RS now until it's too late. The abbreviation isn't any easier to get used to than the name when it's spelled out.*

"I have an idea of what you'll do, and now Felix, if you'll kindly shut the hell up. You pacing around and badgering me like you are a paranoid member of the Machine will not help me out. I'm fucking nervous enough as it is."

"Those balls keep growing, don't they RS. Pretty soon they'll be as big as the elephant man's."

"Cool, you'll have to get me new pants." Felix looks at me and starts laughing. "Okay, I'll exit the room and listen from the distance."

"Thank you."

Felix begins to walk out and pauses one last time to look at me. "You're sure you got this?"

"As sure as I can be. At least I've been working out if I mess up. I might even be able to get a punch in if you try to tackle me down." I smile. Yes, my self confidence has slowly increased due to big efforts by Gia and me to boost it for this crazy mad ass endeavor.

After Felix is out of the room I pick up Otto, my version of a security blanket, and go over to the computers, which are all one sequence away from putting in the codes to hijack the radio frequencies. I do a brief review of the entire system, making sure that everything is in place. It looks as good as it possibly can, and I am sure that it is set up properly.

I quickly move from computer to computer, typing in the codes and then I go to sit down in the chair in front of the broadcasting microphone that is there. This thing is crazy, and undoubtedly meant for the President to deliver a message to the masses in a time of panic. Oddly enough, the bunker makes you think that no one outside of it would even be alive if it was a catastrophic occurrence. If I think I lack toughness at times, President Redman is definitely worse—he is the bottom of the cesspool when it comes to courage and doing the right thing.

I stare at the light that will turn red when I connect to the FABS. Every second seems to take a minute and finally after a real minute passes by it turns red. I am looking into a camera where people will be able to see who I am. My hair is now short and brown again, and I have gained some weight so I still look different. I'm sure the Machine will figure out who I am rather quickly, which is good. They are supposed to in order to make this work. I breathe in and begin to talk as I look into the camera, hoping I make sense and will be gifted with the right words in my message.

I'm here to deliver the citizens of our country a message of hope and inspiration. For far too long now we've been weighted down by the Machine, and many of us out there don't even know what true freedom feels like. I am one of those people and was born into a system that came about due to the selfish laziness of so many people that just assumed they'd always have the America they grew up in. We all know that didn't happen.

Today is the day for action and I don't know how long I'll be on your televisions before I am cut off. I want you to know four things:

- *Number One. We have the numbers to successfully rise against the Machine and reclaim our country and constitution.*
- *Number Two. The bastards of the Machine will kill you if given the chance, but if you*

don't stand up you are surely dying a slow and painful death anyways.

- *Number Three: There will be a means to get you all the weapons you need to protect your loved ones and bring down the MCU or anyone else who stands in your way.*
- *Number Four: I will be with you every step of the way, and will show you how a man of ordinary means can rise up to the occasion and be the Rogue Spartan, the man whose name most of us have whispered in secret circles.*

We've waited far too long for the Rogue Spartan to arrive, and I have finally volunteered. Initially, I chose to do this out of a sense of revenge for those who I love and have lost due to the Machine. But now it is for more. I am doing it because we deserve better. I hold many secrets that I've untapped from the Machine and these secrets show just how afraid they are of us. Redman is a weak man. He, along with the Machine, have developed advanced weapons and contagions to quiet us. We cannot stand for it and bow to their threats to be silent any longer.

It's time to ask yourself this question: What do you have to lose before you stand up and act? Chances are you haven't made a single decision based off of what you'd do the past twenty years.

Everything is based on the consequences of the Machine if they get you, or worse yet, your family.

I know this to be true because we've seen the Redmanitized slowly fade from existence. President Redman cares for nothing aside from keeping power and setting up a regime in which he and his few trusted higher ups are guaranteed lifelong security. Where's our security? We deserve it too. We may not feel it now, but we can take it away from the elitist who scammed the country twenty some years ago. It is our time to act and I will be reaching out to all who want to take our country back. Details will come and once you commit you are fully in.

Look next to you right now and see the faces of those you love. Think of how that face would look if it were trapped in a federal prison work camp for the remainder of its life just for having a voiced opinion. That is what most people in these camps are guilty of—opinions against the Machine.

It's time to stand up against...................

Static sounds out of the microphone and I look up, realizing that the radio signal has been shut off. There is no longer an image of me on the camera. I have done it. Did I say enough? I wonder how it went. Confirmation takes place when Felix, Gia, Fox, Traps, and Pounder all come into the room wearing ecstatic expressions upon their faces.

"It was enough?"

"It was fucking brilliant; enough to scare people into knowing that they must act now!" Felix makes a fist up into the air and slaps me on the back with his free hand. It lands with a thud and a speckle of spit flies from my mouth. Embarrassment.

He charges toward the computer system and pulls the activating core from the center of it. All forms of outward communication technically cease to exist as of now. Still, I do not care at the moment and I am in disbelief that this big step is over. Even more so, I am amazed at how effortlessly the words flew from my mouth. From my perspective I didn't even sound like myself. Maybe it is because of blood rushing to my head and the loud sound of my heartbeat in my ears as I was talking. *Pure adrenaline.*

"I told you he was ready," Gia comments, turning to me to continue her statement. "Your heart made you real, and your intelligence will get you the followers you need. The revolution against the Machine has begun." She is smiling as proudly as if she has just accomplished a major feat herself. Maybe she has…preparing me for what lies ahead cannot be that easy.

"Gia, you were absolutely right. Damn, RS, that was really fantastic. I can't wait to creep out of this shithole in the dark of night and get back to New York and find out what's all happening there."

"How will you know?"

"The signs should be easy to spot. There'll be propaganda documentaries against you all over the burned and embarrassed FABS, and extra MCU on patrol for starters. Who knows what else a desperate man will do, or a desperate man in charge of a bunch of Machine loving higher ups. One thing we know for certain is that any branch of the Machine is a bunch of numb nuts, and they are freaking out right now, my friend. It's fantastic, and if I had a fine bourbon to drink right now I'd do it."

"I bet I can find you one. Don't forget, this place was built for the higher ups. I'll be right back."

I come back ten minutes later with a bunch of glasses in a bag and a bottle of 1980 Parkers Heritage Bourbon. It is completely dusty and very symbolic of the night because it actually comes from a time when there was a semblance of real freedom in the United States. The President had been Ronald Reagan, a man who believed in the power of limited government. "Shall we go to the lounge?"

"The night just keeps getting better," Felix comments. "Pounder, lead everyone to the lounge and pour the fine amber liquid for us all. I need to have one word alone with RS before we celebrate."

Everyone leaves and Felix shuts the door. He doesn't waste any time getting to the point. "You're going to have to really focus on not going stir crazy over the next weeks, maybe even months, RS. Remember, no matter how tempting—no outside communication until I give the all clear."

"I know. I'll be fine."

"It's fucking harder than you think, especially for you since you're a hacker by heart."

"Well, if I try anything or go crazy you can probably be assured that Gia will smack me a good one."

Felix chuckles. "She's a tough one, isn't she."

"Sure is. I'm more afraid of her than Fox, Traps, and Pounder combined."

"I can see why. A Scot with an attitude."

"I have plenty to work on when I can't communicate with the outside world. Don't forget my photographic memory, and all the other documents I have to go over so I can piece the mad puzzle of Richards together. I somehow feel that it is tied to all of this."

"What makes you think that?"

"I'm not sure. Just a hunch that I cannot even begin to prove yet."

"Well, let's go out and celebrate. One of those fine bourbons will probably send you into a deep slumber and a sound night's sleep."

"Not tonight. I am amped up. I think I'll be able to handle two, maybe three."

It turns out that I think I can actually handle five tumblers of bourbon filled to the brim. I have been trying to keep pace with Gia and belief I'm doing a fair job considering my lack of drinking experience. What I really enjoy, more than the taste of the bourbon and the emotional rush from the broadcast, is Gia's company.

She is finally relaxed, giving me the opportunity to ask her more about her. Maybe she won't be as closely guarded as she has previously been when I have attempted it. I am in luck. Gia begins to share stories about growing up in Scotland and it sounds like she has a great life, one that is more free and liberating than what is in the United States. Why come here? I decide to ask.

"Well, it isn't that complicated. Despite the lunacy of the States, and my family thinking I'd gone completely insane I saw an opportunity to be of value here, and a chance to escape."

"Escape what?"

"The prick of an ex-husband I had me there. He was a real bastard."

"You got divorced?"

"No no…nothing like that."

"You're still married?" *That would suck.*

"No, he accidentally ran himself off a high cliff with his little girlfriend. They never found the bodies, but he was eventually ruled dead. Best day of my life, and I don't mind saying it." Gia folds her arms and nods her head. Then she looks over to me and is squinting her eyes a bit. "What do you think of that Ben?"

"Ummm…well…at least you didn't kill him, right?"

Gia busts up laughing at me and slaps my shoulder with her hand. "You are too funny, just too damn funny."

"Now that's something I'm not known for."

"Must be the bourbon. It's a mighty fine blend."

"I've never…" My words are silenced by the full and luscious lips of Gia pressing against my lips. I freeze, unsure how to respond. Admittedly, I don't have a lot of experience in the woman department and Gia is a woman unlike any one I have ever met before.

She pulls away just enough to look me in the eyes. "Now that's a first. You don't want to kiss me then?"

I blush at her bluntness. Who is she kidding? I have definitely thought about kissing her and a whole lot more too. The little spitfire has even seeped into my dreams. "Yah…uuh…" Once again, Gia silences my mumbling with her lips on mine. This time I am ready though and I enjoy every bit of the kiss and don't hold anything back. *I want her so bad…ugh.*

It's hard to say how long we smashing mouth for, but I could keep going on. The problem is that my stomach has startled gurgling. Damn that bourbon. Gia senses something is wrong and she pulls away. "I think the Rogue Spartan is a bit out of sorts. Well, off to bed for you then."

How does she do that? Turn from temptress to bossy doctor in a second flat. I don't argue though and my goal suddenly becomes getting to the safety of my room before I vomit in front of her. I manage to say, "I hope we can pick up on that again sometime. Good night then, Gia." *Bold…hopefully not too bold.*

Gia laughs. "Good night Rogue Spartan."

In the morning when I wake up my head is throbbing like mad and I think it may take me my entire time in isolation to get rid of the headache that is pounding out a tribal beat in my brain. I stumble out to the kitchen and see a note that reads, *Go back to bed. Doctor's orders. ~G.* There is some aspirin and water next to the note. I gladly take the advice and go back to bed where I experience some of the wickedest dreams I have ever had. The best part of them all is that I have conquered in them and haven't fallen short.

Chapter Thirteen: November 10, 2042

I don't realize how right Felix was when he told me that it would not be easy to be isolated without access to information or anything that has been a part of my standard routine for an indefinite period of time. I have no clue what is going on and my aggravation over that definitely shows in my demeanor.

Just like every day, I go to the exercise room and lift some weights, not noticing that Fox walks in to the room too. I am so focused, trying to lift a bigger weight than I've ever attempted before. I am also taking out all my frustration on that weight, but it really isn't helping. To make matters worse, I am actually horny to the point of distraction. It has been six weeks since Gia kissed me, and it hasn't happened again. I am a complete knob about it though, waiting for her to make the move because I am too chicken. Truthfully, I cannot begin to process why she'd pick me out of all the men located at the bunker. And then there is always the most painful option...Gia kissed me because of the bourbon and nothing else. *Ouch.*

"You're doing a great job, but make sure you keep your back straight or you'll strain it." I look around, instantly alert to my surroundings, and snap out of my thoughts.

"Okay. You startled me, Fox. I didn't even hear you come in."

"You're definitely deep in thought."

"Yah, I'm starting to get a bit stir crazy being locked up in this bunker, waiting for some word on what happened as a result of the broadcast. I can't believe Felix hasn't made it back here yet."

I finish my set and look at Fox. He is looking at me with a half assed smile, like he thinks I am full of shit. "What?" I ask.

"I don't mind saying that I think that Felix's lack of response is not your biggest distraction right now. I think it's the one member of our team that isn't like the others, if you know what I mean."

"Do you mean me, the weak ass of the bunch?"

Fox laughs. "Ah…no."

"And I'm guessing you don't mean Otto." I sigh. "It's crazy to be distracted with something like that when all of this madness is now under way, or at least I assume it is. I doubt it's the time to try to see if a relationship works when I have to go out into the world, motivate people, and possibly die. Death would put a damper on things."

"Death can happen any time. Ben, you can't put off living for the now just because you have things to do in the future, even if they are extremely important. That wouldn't make sense, and what would the reward be at the end? Nothing. You've got to embrace the moment, oh mighty Rogue Spartan." Fox laughs again and I shake my head. *I'm glad someone's entertained because it sure as shit isn't me.*

"I'm trying. All things considered, I think I've done an okay job embracing everything the past half year considering how different life has become."

"You didn't like the way life used to be either from what I gather."

"You're correct, but with my friends we got by okay." I decide to pry for information from someone who surely has more experience with women than I do. "So Fox, out of curiosity, if I attempt to go for it with Gia and she punches my lights out, will you protect me?"

"Yah, but I'll be laughing my ass off at the same time."

"That helps the confidence."

"Just go for it—now."

"Now? Isn't that a little bold."

"Not considering how long you've been entertaining the thought," Fox says. He is not going to let me off the hook. Of course I know he is right. I should go for it.

Twenty minutes later I am showered and going to hunt Gia down. It shouldn't be too hard to find her in the bunker. It's not all that big. She'll either be reading a book in the lounge or sorting through the information that we stare at each and every day to act like we are doing our part to keep busy. I don't like to admit the thoughts that have been wafting into my mind because they seem very disloyal to my friends, but getting revenge on Richards is starting to take a back seat to getting the message of Dr. Jay Secton out there. I am hoping that I can play a part in really kicking Redman and his cronies out of office, and reclaiming a government for the people. My friends would love that and be even more surprised if they discovered I am an intricate part of that plan.

I am right. Gia is in the room, and I walk in there ready to act. Gia turns her head immediately upon my entrance. "Hey there. Your workout was nice?"

"It was," I say. I walk right up to Gia as she is moving something around on the sounding board we have created.

She turns around to find me standing right behind her and definitely in her space.

I gently put my hand up under her chin and lean in and kiss her without holding anything back. I don't cast any doubts in my mind, or bother to hide just how much I respond to her. I just keep kissing her passionately and she is letting me. *Yes! She's letting me!*

Every part of my body is stimulated by this kiss and Gia is moving her lips on mine greedily. I can feel her breasts pressed into my chest and they feel so good. My mind wanders to what they'd look like. I bet they are as silky smooth as the rest of her skin, plump, and luscious.

I don't want to stop, but Gia pulls away. She gives me that quizzical look that has become all too familiar the past months. "It's about time then. What took you so long?"

"Chicken shit. No other excuse."

"An honest man then. I like it."

"That's good to hear. You know, you really are damn beautiful."

"Are you going to go and get all sappy on me then?"

"Not me. I'm a tough guy. Well okay, a sensitive getting tougher guy, but trust me. It's a good mix."

"I think I believe you."

"I look forward to when you know you can believe me."

Otto runs in to the room and starts swatting at my pant leg. That's his little sign that he has to take care of some business. I sigh. Well, it was nice while it lasted.

"I have to go tend to Otto."

"All right then, Ben. Next time, don't take so long to act."

I smile. "As you request." I leave the room and my smile is so big that I swear it's stretching to my ears. My cheeks are actually hurting and I can't get it off.

With Otto under arm, I walk down the hall. "Otto, I finally did it. Are you proud of me, boy?" He nudges my arm. "I'll take that as a yes."

"And why is Otto proud of you?"

I whip my head around and see Felix standing there at the edge of one of the apartment rooms. "Damn. You startled me, but I'm glad to see you, Felix. Let me tend to Otto, and then track you down. I want information."

"Well, I have it to give. Meet me in the lounge in ten."

I am waiting in the lounge in ten minutes, along with everyone else. We all look eager and anxious about what Felix is about to share. So much is riding on this moment and the news h e has. The next set of plans really cannot be made until we know our starting point after the broadcast.

Gia sits down next to me and Fox winks at me. She notices it, and I get a bit embarrassed. *No time for that now.* She doesn't seem to care though, which is something amazing about her. She does not show hesitation when it comes to following her instincts.

Felix decides to make a grand entrance and walks in with his arms extended wide. He's sporting a grand smile. "My friends, I trust you've all fared well. From the looks of it, you all seem to be doing fairly well considering the isolation."

"It works better for some of us than others," Pounder says, grinning like a Cheshire cat.

Felix responds like he knows exactly what Pounder is talking about. "Whatever keeps our boy motivated."

I am not too happy to be having innuendos about my apparently obvious feelings tossed about like I am not here. I hope I haven't been making an ass out of myself. I interrupt the banter. "Why don't we get down to business. What's happening out there, and did the broadcast work?"

"Glad to see the excitement, RS. And to answer your questions—the broadcast has exploded like a laser gun tagging a petroleum tank. The response has been incredible, and my network has been out there preparing people for action. Small militia group formation, physical training, and other relevant means of protecting themselves from the MCU when they go all postal on them. It's nothing short of brilliant."

"And what about the Machine? What's been going on with them?" I ask, wondering if I'll ever be able to leave the bunker again without being in danger.

"They have done just as we expected. No surprise—they are not known for real creativity and thinking outside the box. However, you do have someone that's climbed the ladders of the Machine that does have some knowledge of you."

"Who?"

"Richards. He must have had some serious shit on a good many higher ups because he suddenly finds himself being the next in command—the big old VP."

"Holy crap. So the hunches were right about him. He is a climber. Does he have it out for me?" *That is some quest for power that Richards has embarked on.*

"Hard to say…maybe. He is personally leading a committee whose sole purpose is to capture you alive, and bring you in."

"At least they don't want to capture me dead yet."

"Don't be so sure that alive is better, RS. You see, they want to make an example out of you and it's one that is meant to scare any individual who dares show defiance or stand up against the Machine. You are the very opposite of them in their eyes—the leader of a rogue movement, and the anti-Machine."

"They acknowledge me as the leader?" I cannot believe that is accurate, even though it is the ultimate objective.

"Yes, and it's time for you to act like a leader. I've taken the liberty of drafting the next two stages of the plan. I am assuming you'll be agreeable."

"Well, what are they, Felix?"

"Another broadcast, and then a little publicity tour."

"Publicity tour. That seems like a strange move considering I'm undercover."

"Can't stay here forever. The people will demand to see you in the fray with them."

"And that's the way it should be." I know that I cannot do this without putting myself out there, or else I'm no better than the Redmanitized. "Will the broadcast be from here again?"

"It will, and then we'll be hauling ass out of here the second it's done, or cut off. That's when you'll be starting your publicity tour. It's going to be intense, and probably insane. You'd better be ready because none of us know what'll happen." Felix claps his hands together, salivating at the thought of the chaos. He gets a rush from those things and oddly enough it provides me with confidence that I can go extreme if I need to and be all right…maybe even better than that.

"Are we all a part of the tour?" Gia asks.

"Absolutely Gia. You've all proven that you a damn great team, and with Fox, Pounder, and Traps you'll have the immediate muscle you need to maneuver through just about any situation that the Machine may throw at you if they catch your lead."

"Not against one of those laser guns," I say. I've been very aware of this and how those guns make it easy to eliminate any problem before it gets too close. I have been working really hard in my spare time at designing a device that should jam the laser in theory. I just haven't been able to test it because of having to be off the radar. I need some codes from LaserMachination, and a few other places to make sure my frequencies are aligned. I've never been a solid engineer, but desperate times call for a little extra effort. Cal's random notes from SOURCE have also helped me out.

"Okay then, let's enjoy some food, have some friendly conversation, and prepare everything we'll need for a departure from here that's best compared to a bat flying straight out of hell."

Felix's idea sounds great to me. I have already started tossing around some ideas for the next broadcast and hope they deliver an impact message like the last one did.

I go to my room for a bit and stare in the round mirror on my tan wall. I am staring at me and I cannot believe it's actually me, Ben Danrick—Rogue Spartan—whatever. I've bulked up some and my hair is growing out rapidly. I am different; more confident and possibly ready for all this. It's quite the revelation, although it's been a transformation that's taken a half year for me to morph into.

Chapter Fourteen: December 1, 2042
I don't know how Felix does it, but the guy has ways. I'd mentioned my idea for jamming the lasers briefly the other day and talked about how I couldn't quite complete it for a test run due to not having access to anything via the Intranet. He walks into the office, where I'm focused on preparing for the next broadcast, which is about two hours away, and tosses some numbers at me.

"What's this?" I ask, looking at the paper. I know the question is redundant because I can tell exactly what the codes are—they are laser synchronization techniques. I just cannot believe my eyes.

"All you need to do is ask, my friend." Felix is grinning, loving the confused look I'm sporting. "Can you plug those in now? Perhaps we could do a quick little test run."

"I don't think it's a good idea to test a laser here in the bunker. You never know what'll happen."

"Well, how about in the fresh air. It'd be pretty fucking amazing to know that your invention worked before we actually go out and are face to face against some crazy ass dude and his laser gun."

"Outside?" I am in. I have always thought that I didn't get enough fresh air when I was in my apartment, but this bunker makes the apartment look like a tropical island full of fresh breeze.

"It'll take me ten minutes to program, and then I'll be set. Get a target, and a gun."

"You're set for the broadcast, right?"

I nod. "I'll feel a lot better about my tour if I know this laser jammer works. Okay, leave me to it, and I'll meet you by the entrance in 10."

Plugging in the codes is fairly easy, and I watch the sequence of red, orange, and blue lights move about, processing the information. The sound of the jammer buzzes slightly, showing that it is aligning itself to meet the specifications I input. "Please may this work," I mumble to Otto, who's looking at me suspiciously.

I leave the office and run into Gia. "Where you going?" she asks.

"Out to test the laser jammer. I can't wait."

"Cool, I'm going to watch then."

"Will Felix let you?"

"Surely you are kidding. Do you think you're the only one of the team who can operate that. I'm a girl with skills, some of them you're yet to find out about, but still…Alright then?"

"Alright!" I grin, loving the intoxicating tone of Gia's toughness. It's crazy, like the type of talk that mythical comic book super heroes say…and not the Machine's version of cool—Captain Fairly, Advocate for All. It's legitimate cool.

Five minutes later, I'm breathing fresh air, getting ready to test the first thing of real significance that I've ever invented (partial credit given to Amy, Cal, and Max) and also just over an hour away from another broadcast. It's an exciting day by any stretch of the imagination for me—quite possibly the most event filled one ever.

I'm wearing a vest to help protect me from the laser in case there's an accident. Part of me is thinking I am not as valuable as I was starting to believe because I'm definitely at risk from getting lacerated into prairie fertilizer. Right in front of me is the target. It's a dummy holding a fake laser gun and its pointing at Felix. Even from a hundred feet away I can see the maniacal grin on his face as he picks up the gun and fires.

Despite me asking for a warning before he fires, Felix makes it clear that people don't get warnings and that I cannot effectively gauge if the jammer works with one. I gulp and pray.

A small red circle with a white ring starts growing larger and I press the white button in the center of the small black fob that I'm holding—the jammer. It seems like eternity is passing by, but in reality it's only a nano-second. I don't take my eyes of the laser, hoping I can duck if worse comes to worse. *Yah, right!* It seems like long drawn out thoughts are processing in my mind, and just when I think I've really messed up and cost me my life I see the red light reflect and go off to the right.

Okay, this is good, but then again, this is also bad. An innocent bystander or ally could get killed with refraction. Damn…it's not what it needs to be yet.

Felix is shouting and charging toward me, waving his laser gun in the air, and moving surprisingly quick for his thick clunky boots and long weighted canvas jacket.

"Awesome…ab-so-lute-ly fucking awesome!"

"Not really." I am definitely distracted by the refraction. I don't know what I was thinking would happen exactly, but I thought the laser would just disintegrate…for lack of a better word. I know nothing goes away completely— basic physics—but I thought the form would transfer to something else, something that didn't kill like that particular laser intensity did.

"Come on, why not?" Felix is looking at me like I am the one that's impossible to figure out.

"It refracted, which means that whoever was standing to my left would have been the recipient of the deadly laser blow."

"My friend, it is dandy that you are all sweet and humanitarian about it and all, but you are the asset here. You are the one that needs to be alive in the end. For my purposes, your jammer worked. It may seem harsh, it may seem cold, but it is what it is."

"If I hadn't thought of inventing it you wouldn't be able to say that."

"But you did think of it, and somewhere in the back of your mind, you or one of your little hacking friends, saw the need for the basis of the research. Deal with it, and get your ass back in the bunker to get ready for the broadcast."

I look at Felix, startled and annoyed by his reprimanding tone. I look at him and can't tell if he'd dicking around with me or being serious. I somehow think it's a combination of both and I go back in. Regardless of his intentions, I do have a broadcast to put out in an hour. Then, it's adios bunker and hello to Rogue Spartan on the run. Me and my posse.

With a half hour to go before broadcast time I am waiting in the room, and Felix comes in to bring the activating core he'd snatched out of the computer system just after the first broadcast was cut off. Gia's next to me and she is surprisingly quiet, perhaps afraid that she'll ruin my concentration if she talks. Is she nervous? Nah, can't be...I'm the one who is nervous once again. *Will I ever get used to this?*

"Five, four, three, two, one...go get 'em, RS." Felix plugs in the activating core and takes a step back. He stands in the corner with his arms crossed. Apparently he isn't leaving for this broadcast.

My face shows itself on the screen. The light to indicate audio is functioning is there. This is going to be interesting because I am interrupting President Redman's

State of the Nation Address, which he'll portray as all lovely. I don't think I'm too lovely in his perspective.

I'm sure you've all been touched by the endearing words of old Redman tonight, but I am here to tell you words of truth—not words of a propaganda loving and desperate man, a man who will destroy friend or family if he perceives them as a threat. So, if you consider yourself a person with a brain...listen up. You won't want to miss this.

President Redman has been taking desperate measures to stop certain people he perceives as a threat and he has incorporated the help of a man now known to you all as Mr. Richards, your Vice President.

The reason that I was cast into the role I am in now—the Rogue Spartan—is actually something that Mr. Richards indirectly led me to. I'm not sure why and I doubt it was his intention, but it has happened. You see, every person that Mr. Richards targeted in his aggressive climb up in the world of the higher up's was someone he had me investigate in some capacity. It was only when he asked me to turn information over on my friends that it all stopped.

Do I have regrets? No. The people that have been taken out of the picture were insignificant and a bunch of ass kissers whose biggest thrill was making the average American's life hell and lifting themselves up while they did it.

I say no more. Today is the day everything changes and today is the day that the Rogue Spartan comes out of hiding. I am going to go out and meet with those of you who have started these amazing militia's and resistance orders—ready to turn off the Machine and restore the constitution...

"Connection lost," Felix says. "Impressive and stinging—just my style, RS. Let's get the hell out of here."

Five minutes later, I'm running with Otto into the garage of the bunker and Felix, Gia, Otto, Traps, Fox, and Pounder are with me. We jump into the black terrain multi-functional vehicle that's in the bunker—a prototype that is meant for the sole use of President Redman or someone of higher authority. We won't be able to be in the vehicle for long because it's too identifiable; however, it's also a completely protected off the radar vehicle with a direct link to the MCU Chief Commander in it.

We blaze across the plain, traveling surprisingly smoothly at 100 mph, charging for the woods that are about two miles ahead. Once we are in there we can slow it down because we'll be covered, and not as visible. No one lives in the woods, as they are still protected by the government because of a rare beetle they found in there, named the Alinsaul Beetle. Despite the protection, the beetle died off anyways, as it was indigenous to certain parts of Russia. Well today, the Alinsaul Beetle is helping us make our get away, despite the fact that it'll never know it. One dumb ass law that has turned into a somewhat shocking benefit for us.

Once we're in the safety of the woods we all stop for a moment. The first part of the escape is over and now we can move a bit more slowly and more inconspicuously as a result. There are humming noises, barely visible, coming from the distance—in the direction in which the bunker would be. Felix stands on the hood of the vehicle and pulls out his binoculars.

"The place is crawling with Reverb Choppers, and Land Hoverers compliments of the Machine. We made it, and boy are they going to be pissed."

"Will they be able to see tire tracks in the field showing them where we headed?" I ask, hoping that isn't the case. We should have thought of that.

"Nope," Felix says casually. "You see, this beauty of a machine was designed with low lying turbines that move in the opposite direction it does. It literally blows the evidence away. Of course it was meant for people to not track Redman, but this result is a bit more fun, wouldn't you say?"

"I would."

Fox suddenly pulls out his gun and aims to a thicket of brush in the woods. Pounder puts his hand up to his mouth, signaling for us all to be quiet.

We all stare in the direction that Fox is pointing his gun at and look. What's there? A minute later, a jack rabbit jumps out, startling Fox almost as much as he startled it. I don't mind that I laughed out loud because I didn't think anything startled the big bastard…apparently bunnies do.

Chapter Fifteen: December 10, 1042

I have been out of the bunker for over a week now, and have visited three cities: Bozeman, MT; Pueblo, CO; and Duluth, MN. There are three more to go on the tour. At each location I've been amazed at how the underground information network has set these meetings up. They've all been going so smoothly with no incidents from the Machine, MCU, or any other form of retaliation.

Every night we stay some place different. A few nights we've had the luxury of a hotel room because we offered cash—a luxury to small business owners. Their silence is easily purchased. Other nights, we camp out under the stars and sleep on the hard ground. That is not ideal for me and Otto makes it worse. He always crawls down to the bottom of the sleeping bag to stay warm and then squirms around because I accidentally move and make him uncomfortable.

I would have thought there would be an abundance of alone time on this tour, but the only time I get alone is when I actually have to go use the bathroom. This means that I've gotten nowhere with Gia and we haven't really had a chance to do anything to explore our boundaries a bit further. Maybe it's best that I'm not distracted by her during this time, but dang…I sure want to be.

Every day that there is a meeting I am fortunate to manage a way to channel that guy hidden in me who can talk to people face to face and make sense. I don't think I'm rambling, and whenever I get stuck or an unknown question is entered into the equation Felix jumps in. I don't know if the guy's telepathic or something, but he seems to be able to effortlessly respond to any question anyone asks.

Most of the meetings have averaged about one hundred people, which is a lot more than I thought I'd be seeing. They've traveled at great risk to the meeting locations, some even crossing state lines—a big illegal act that can get you tossed into a work camp without an opportunity to explain.

People's questions for me are usually the same. They want to know:
- What's the plan?
- What if it fails?
- How will they stay in the loop?
- How do we know that we don't have any Machine infiltrators?
- How can they ensure their families remain protected?

My answers are always the same, but they resonate with truth, sincerity, and conviction, letting people know that:

- For now, the plan is to get the forces together that have the tools and technology necessary to go up against the Machine. There will be risks, and there is no avoiding that. This is not a game, it's a very real situation and will likely have some harsh consequences. Some people will die, and that can't be avoided, but rest assured, I will not back down until I am either dead myself, or have beaten down the Machine, and toppled what was. Then, it'll be time to restore the constitution.

- If this plan fails it really is just moving up the inevitable—a loss of any sense of individual identity, and no guarantees that you can protect the ones you love from anything. It's either risk for possible reward, or silence for life.

- The communication network consists of leaders from 100 quadrants on the mainland, and they will have the means to communicate with me or Felix, situation depending, and receive instructions. It's the communication leaders that will find ways to get that information to you.

- We cannot guarantee we don't have any infiltrators, but we do have a very advanced system of being able to detect people's intentions, and methods of looking into their histories on the Intranet, and even the Internet from when it existed. Our Research and Confirmation Specialist is exceptional, and a trained psychologist with a proven history of being devoted to the original US Constitution.

- The best way to ensure that your families remain protected is to teach them how to live off the grid, defend themselves, don't act irrationally, and be honest with them about what is going on. You cannot fight on their behalf without them knowing that you are a part of the Anti-Machine.

Each meeting ends with a task list that is handed out, and from there, you have to rely on the attendees to make sure they take that information back to their quadrants and start implementing it the best they can. The smaller areas are at a significant advantage because the MCU doesn't patrol them as heavily, and their officials are not the most skilled of the MCU either.

* * *

Today is the meeting in Chicago. It's the largest area we've been to and it is a bit unnerving. There are so many people around and it's hard to really monitor all of them. Still, according to Felix, this is necessary. He hasn't led me astray so far, and to question him is...well, pointless. He does what he does and nobody, not even me, can change his mind it seems.

"This is the biggest crowd yet," I say to Gia, who looks uneasy. Her eyes keep assessing the room. We are in an old warehouse by the wharf and make our way to it by taking a small paddle boat just as night falls. It's now 9 p.m. and dark. The huge warehouse is dimly lit so it doesn't cast light or cause suspicion to the numerous MCU that patrol near the area. This group has people from Wisconsin, Michigan, and Iowa, and Illinois, which is why it's in Chicago. It's the most central and safe for those who are crossing the state lines.

"I estimate about a three hundred head count. What's your guess?" Gia asks.

"Closer to four hundred by the time everyone files in."

"How are they all getting in unseen?" I wonder.

"Felix devised some system. It seems to be working, but it's driving me mad, is what it is doing, Ben."

I smile. Gia is the only person who still calls me Ben. The confirmation that my identity hasn't been totally erased is somehow reassuring. For a moment I reflect on what Cal, Amy, and Max would say about this. I can hear their responses so vividly in my mind.

Gia is looking at me with a faint smile, I realize. "What?"

"You were thinking about your friends, weren't you?"

"How'd you know that?"

"You just get a certain look…that's all. I know it must be hard not having them around."

"It is, but everyone has to learn to live without people they care about, I guess. You have."

"I assure you, my situation was considerably different, and those around me were wankers and fools."

"You never met Max. You'd categorize him like that in an instant, I'd bet."

Gia smiles and grabs my hand gently. She squeezes it and it makes me feel good, instantly calming my rising nerves.

The time to start the meeting has come and I am ready to go and talk to the largest crowd yet. They are very quiet, considering the size of the audience, and I can almost sense their anticipation. Its times like this that you can understand how silence does have the ability to be more powerful than boisterous rumblings from a worked up group of people.

I walk out and the shadow of the yellow dimming light hanging from the ceiling of the warehouse falls down on my body. I feel like I'm ready to perform a one man show on Broadway and I look out. I don't see any faces, but I am listening closely and I can hear people breathing ever so slightly.

Thank you for what you risk to be here today. With every place that I've visited the intensity of the Anti-Machine movement has increased, and by the time we all leave here today it will be even more so. Within this room there are a committed group of people that want more for their families, for their futures....for America.

One lone guy shouts out, "Yah." He's immediately quieted, either by his own doing or someone close by. I can't see.

This movement may have called me its leader, but I am merely a part of the equation, the catalyst if you will, and you all are the solution. Without you and your willingness to sacrifice this cannot happen. You are the Anti-Machine every bit as much as me and everything you sacrifice just to be here tonight is evidence of that.

If we stand together, do not waiver on principle and say, 'No! I will not accept a life dictated for me, but one that I dictate of my own free accord,' we will come out of this prosperous, wiser, and with newfound knowledge of the heart that we can be proud to pass down to our ancestors. The founding fathers of America would be proud to see their beliefs still exist within their child—the people of America.

It's not the time to think about where it went wrong. This is the time to think about how to make it better. Yes, it'll take time, and no...it will not happen easily, but it can happen. That's why the Machine has been acting so irrationally.

I frustrate them more than anything because there is nothing from my past for them to threaten my silence with. What I have is a vision of what can be and that is scarier than anything to them because they know they can't steal it. They know they will never be able to take it. And despite their efforts, the Machine knows that they cannot steal what is in the hearts and minds of men that value true freedom.

I pause. My heart is beating rapidly and I am amped up. I reach for a bottle of water and take a drink before continuing. I still wish I could see the faces out there, but despite their invisible features I know they are listening, and they are attentive to what I have to say.

There is a group of people with me that can help you get everything in order that you must in order to help in our ultimate objective—stopping Redman from recreating the United States of America any further. Can it ever be what it was before? Probably not; however, it can be a smarter country and a more aware country. We cannot ask for or expect more than that.

You'll see some information being handed out to all of you right now. Guard this with your life and never lose sight of it. You'll see that it is on paper, as I know that some of the greatest assets to the Machine don't have the ability to use the authoritarian approved Intranet, or the ability to look at something without the fear of the ITC laying down its fury on you. This is the safest way and therefore a way that the Machine is not as likely to understand. They've stopped thinking like most of man long ago and have been fueled by a vision that their egos perceive as reality.

Here...today...right now...this is reality. This is the Anti-Machine and this is what will soon come to be. It will rewrite the history books of our culture in a light that shows that we did care, we did fight to correct our wrongs, and we did it the right way.

Force through war is nothing new to man and it is not new to the United States either. It may not always be necessary, but it always draws attention and we have definitely drawn the attention of Redman and his Redmanitized following. They fear us and they know that we have something they could never hope to have—truly devout people to the cause. We are not here because we've been paid to be here or will benefit monetarily from it. We are here because we choose to be here and we want to make a difference. And today, that shall start.

Thank you.

Just as quickly as I'd shown up in the dim yellow light, I faded into the darkness. I don't know what had come over me, but I feel like it is the best address I've given to date. I am getting the hang of this.

"Well then, you've been holding back on some of that talk, haven't 'ya?" Gia asks. Before I can answer she leans in and kisses me passionately. So, she was inspired and apparently I've inspired myself too because despite the moment and the intensity of the situation I am aroused. Gia's kiss warms me and reminds me of just how exciting a life without the Machine's restrictions can be—will be.

Fox, Pounder, and Traps large frames are visible in the back of the room despite the darkness and I pity the person that would ever entertain messing with one of them. I know I wouldn't. I can see Traps hand go up to his ear. Someone is talking with him and he nods. Before I know it the sound of a rapid fire gun—one with bullets—starts to echo out and I look around.

Damn it, I can't see anything and don't know what's going on. Gia is looking around too. There's no sign of Felix and now I only see the shadows of Fox and Pounder in the background. Is Traps down or is he moving somewhere. What's going on?

"Come here. We've got to duck," Gia snaps.

I take her lead and we duck down behind an old oil barrel, hoping it'll cover our bodies enough. It's in the darkness so it's not easily visible. Suddenly, a large sound comes from the tin ceiling of the warehouse and a portion of the roof disintegrates, casting a large light from high powered solar flares into the warehouse.

I can't see and I'm trying to shield my eyes from the intensity. It looks like a bright white light—what you'd imagine the entrance to heaven being. I'm squinting, hoping that Gia and I are still hidden despite the intensity. Surely it must be hurting those who are firing the guns eyes.

People are screaming; some in pain and some in anger. Groups of people are charging each other. Suddenly, the back door is busted down and I see a familiar silhouette walking into the warehouse. It's Mr. Richards and he is wearing dark glasses. His goons must be wearing them too—that's how they can see even with the intensity of the flares.

I whisper to Gia. "That's Richards."

"We've got to get out of here. Come on."

"How will we do that?" I cannot think of how I can possibly escape this madness right now. Is it wrong for me to flea and abandon those who came here to support the Rogue Spartan?

Gia doesn't say a word and points toward the door that Mr. Richards walked through a minute earlier. It's swinging open and there is a vehicle parked in front of it. It is official government black and looks like the best chance of escaping intact. I wonder if anyone is standing outside. It seems odd to not have someone there if they are raiding the rest of the warehouse.

I see Mr. Richards looking in my direction, and I hesitate, wondering if he sees me. Yet, he's not the guy with the ability to kill. He gives the orders and that somehow makes him less threatening even if he is a man of power.

Gia reaches into her jacket pocket and pulls out a small semi-automatic pistol. "Come on. There's no time. Stay behind me."

I listen. She's obviously been through this before and I haven't been involved in anything this intense. We make a mad dash out the back door, and Gia whips her head around the corner, looking left and right. She must think it's all clear because she doesn't say a word.

"Get in!" I listen and slide into the back seat, which is the only open door. Gia runs around the corner toward the driver's door and hops over something before opening the door. She puts the vehicle into drive as she's closing the door and guns it. "Stay ducked, Ben. I know this is bullet proof, but I don't want to take chances."

"What about Felix and the guys?"

"They'll be fine. It's you we must worry about then."

Gia is one quick driver and I can't believe how much my body is swaying back and forth as she speeds through the alleyway on the one side of the pier, maneuvering us into the busy Chicago traffic. I can't see what's going on, but I hear shouts and horns. Even for someone driving a government vehicle her driving is noticeable. The authoritarians always drive like dicks, really irritating those who have option number one and only—the bus.

Finally, we are out of town. I don't know how long it's taken, but Gia pulls over and tells me to get up. I'm glad to do so and my head is throbbing from hitting the seat when we crossed bumps in the road.

"We can't be keeping this car very well, now can we?" Gia comments. It's awkward, like she's filling some sort of gap.

"I suppose not. Richards' car is definitely visible, starting with the VP seal on its side. Odd that they'd mark it though, don't you think?"

"I was thinking that too, Ben."

"You know, I know you have certain skills and I'm not questioning them," I begin. "So, don't get me wrong, but didn't that seem a bit too easy, too convenient?"

"I was thinking the same thing," Gia responds, looking at me. "What do you think it means then?"

"I don't know, but I almost feel like Richards is trying to help me. That doesn't make much sense though, but let's face it. I am not practiced in the skills of escape in high gun power altercations."

"You got that right then."

"I should be insulted, but something about that accent takes the edge off."

"It's just a fact, Ben. Nothing more."

"I am thinking that I need to talk to Richards in order to help the cause."

Gia looks at me. I can tell she is wondering if I'm back on my revenge for my friends, but this time I am not focused on that. Something is telling me that I can get something I need from Richards, even if I can't pinpoint what it is yet. "If you're sure, then we'll do it then."

I smile. We end up spending the night hidden under a thicket of tall oak trees in a field and lying sprawled out in the spacious back seat of the VPs car. It's not the most comfortable, yet it feels very comfortable because of Gia. I could get used to this.

Chapter Sixteen: December 31, 2042

Okay, I'm on the run so I can't be too particular about where I have to lay my head at night, but man, this really sucks. I'm in an old barn and even Gia's company is not enough to make me realize just how miserable I am. Otto is the only one enjoying himself. He loves to chase after all the little field mice and bark at the occasional bat that swoops down in the middle of the night.

We have no communication right now and no idea where Felix is, or if he'll find us. Gia says she has an idea on how to get a hold of him, but she can't do anything until we get to the city. In this case that city is DC because that's where Richards makes his home these days. Getting to him will not be easy, but it must be done.

"How far do you think we can get on foot in this winter climate?" I ask Gia. I cannot imagine how I am going to make my way to DC from rural Illinois in the middle of winter. It's colder than usual, subzero already, and the wind has been howling like mad. The little bit of food we so resourcefully got before having to surrender the VP vehicle is starting to run low too.

"I think we'll have to thumb it." Gia says this like it's no big deal. I think differently.

"That cannot be a safe idea. Everyone probably knows who I am now."

"That doesn't mean that everyone is against you. Don't forget that."

"Okay. How will we disguise me just to make sure?" I am not as resourceful as Gia yet and cannot fathom pulling this type of thing off on our own.

"It's entirely possible that I'm recognizable now, Ben. It fucking pisses me off, it does."

"Sorry I dragged you into this."

"I made my own decisions and I'll deal with the consequences." Gia crosses her arms and tilts her head. "You know, I've been thinking about what you said…about this all being too easy thus far. It does seem odd."

"You think Richards is up to some alternate plan?"

"Likely, but…"

"But what, Gia?"

"Oh nothing." Gia changes the subject on me and I know she is holding back from blurting something out to me. What is it? Doesn't she trust me?

"Well, we should take off at dawn tomorrow. Maybe we can walk to a café or diner that serves breakfast to the trucker crowd. That may be the easiest way to assess things."

"Okay. That'll also allow us to stow away if we decide we don't want to ask anyone for help, won't it?"

"Yah, but how will we know they are heading in the right direction...to DC?"

"You've got to be resourceful, Ben. Their license plates, and approved state passage stickers will show which trucks are heading that way. We'll target the one that will get us closest. We know it won't be DC specifically, as they will not allow large vehicles within the city—fears of bombs and people hostile to the Machine."

"Okay," I say. I'm not really sure what else to say and I am suddenly feeling awkward around Gia. The familiar feeling of annoyance and frustration that I've always gotten on occasion seeps into me and I wish I could see the solutions that are before me. I'm better, but damn, I have a long way to go.

Suddenly my mood turns sour and I feel fed up with all of this—sick of it. I don't want to be the Rogue Spartan and I think that the cause would be better served with a naturally fearless person like Gia. Hell, even Felix would be a better choice. He gets things done and is connected. Me? I'm a hacker who got busted and ever since I've been on the run, making life crazier than what I'm comfortable with. I may not be a good many things, but I am someone who is aware of my limits and I'm on the verge of crossing the line of what's feasible in my life.

I head toward the door of the old barn.

"Where you going?"

"I'm just going outside for a bit. I need to think some things out." I plan on running and getting the hell out of here. Gia doesn't need me to survive and I'm an idiot if I think she could really be content with a guy like me, a guy who isn't smart enough to go the distance.

"So running away will solve it all then, will it? What about those who believe in you?"

I freeze in my tracks. How does Gia know I'm thinking that? It annoys me even further.

"Look, you don't need me here, and you can be a better Rogue Spartan than I ever could hope to be. If you think it's so important, do it!" I pick up my backpack and Otto is staring at me. I add in, "Keep Otto too. He'll probably be safer."

"You're a wanker," Gia says. She turns away and I walk out the door. It takes all my effort to shut the old barn door again because a big draft of wind is resisting me. I finally shut it and I look out across the field. I can see a few vehicles on a highway and it's probably a mile away. It's hard to say with all the white snow. It's already late afternoon so I'm going to have to move fast to get to that highway.

I've walked over the crunch and crusted snow for about a hundred yards. Each step echoes out across the plain and I am already feeling like a complete ass for the way I treated Gia. She's here with me to help, not to deal with me being an asshole just because I'm collapsing under the pressure of all this shit. I am a wanker, as Gia so fondly reminds me on occasion. What a wanker is exactly, I don't know. You don't really need to know to get the message that it is not a compliment.

After a brief pause I turn around and start trudging back to the barn. I'm already cold and realize that it was not too smart of me to just put a jacket on and not properly prepare myself for a trek across the frozen tundra. I take another step and my foot doesn't stop. It breaks through the icy layer of snow and keeps going downward, causing me to fall right down. Crack. My entire body is under the snow and I can feel ice cold water running by my boots.

I try to pull myself up and every time I do the thin layer of snow just breaks more. All the snow has obviously drifted over a stream that runs through the field and I am screwed. I cannot yell for help because there's no way that Gia or anyone else can hear me. The wind is blowing in my face and sending my voice off into a million different directions.

I turn my back so my face isn't against the wind. Maybe I can walk toward the place where I fell in. After all, that was solid ground. Then I can hurry back to the barn and unthaw before I get sick. I try to move and find that I'm getting nowhere fast. I'm so damn tired I can barely make myself stay awake or focused. I have no clue how long I've been here.

"Grab this, you wanker," a voice calls out. I turn around and see Gia looking at me. Her eyes are intense and she's trying to act pissed, but I see the fear in her eyes. It's unmistakable. She tosses me a rope with a slip knot tied around one end. She throws it like a lasso and I find myself temporarily in awe of yet another one of her skills.

The rope lands by me and I'm shivering. I can't talk and Gia calls out commands, starting with saving my energy. "Just put the rope around you," she adds.

I get it around me and under my arm pits. Now Gia is rearing back, beginning to tug on me. I try to help, but I can't feel my feet and I'm not even sure if they're touching ground. Gia keeps pulling and I'm fading in and out, knowing that I must try to not become dead weight. It's so hard. Eventually, I feel my body sliding along the ground like it's a sled.

Gia comes up to me and flips me on my back. She reaches down behind me and latches her hands under my arms and begins to walk backwards, dragging me across the snow. Gia's yelling at me. "Stay focused, Ben. Stay with me. Come on. Don't you dare fall asleep, you wanker."

I look at her and I think I nod. It's so hard to tell because I cannot feel a single thing on my body. I can't even tell if my heart's beating. My eyes are glassed over with ice and everything looks foggy. I try to close them, but they won't cooperate. Eventually Gia sets me down and I can hear her opening the large door to the barn. She has to kick snow in front of it to act as a stopper so it doesn't keep slamming shut on her.

Gia drags me in and quickly shuts the door. She leaves me right at the spot where she set me and begins to undress me. "We've got to get you out of these clothes, Ben. Come on…stay awake…stay awake."

I'm not sure what's going on, but I feel something prickling my skin, making it itch badly. I can hardly breathe and I feel the heat of a warm body next to me. I look over and see Gia staring at me. Her shoulders are bare and I suddenly realize that I'm naked…her too. I manage to whisper out. "Thank you."

Gia looks relieved that I am talking. She leans in and gives me a soft kiss on the lips. I smile. "Did you do that just to get me naked then?"

"Why are you naked?"

"You had hypothermia, and well…I am the warmest thing in this barn. Otto wanted to help, but he started shivering the second he curled up by you. As you can see, he's been keeping watch though." Gia points to a spot just to the right of me and I strain to lift my head up. Otto's sitting there staring at me. His big brown eyes look like they are afraid to blink.

"Otto," I say. He runs over and nuzzles my cheek with his nose. "I'm okay, boy. I'm okay."

"You're really not okay yet," Gia interrupts. "You are still rather cold, and we have no way to dry your clothes out. And, if I know anything at all—which I definitely do—you're going to get a fever from all of this. Your body is wiped out."

"I don't think I'm going to get a fever," I say.

"Don't argue with me," Gia says, standing up and showing her in her naked glory. I cannot believe how amazing every curve of her body is. She is incredible. I know I'm staring, but I can't stop. I don't ever recall a time when a woman, one around me anyways, was so comfortable in her own skin—literally.

"I won't argue," I say. Gia walks away and I can hear her doing something. I'm not sure what, but I must fall asleep because I wake up later and see that it is dark in the barn. The only light is coming from an old oil lamp that Gia had found. She has it hanging from a rafter and I watch her briefly. She's deep in thought, staring up toward the loft. I wonder what she's thinking.

I stand up and realize that I'm still naked due to a lack of dry clothes. I can't stay naked forever unless I don't plan on leaving the barn and that can't happen. I see a ratty old wool blanket by me and I reach to grab it. I keep looking at Gia the entire time. Why? I'm not sure. I just hope she doesn't look over and see me standing here naked because I am not feeling all too great right now. I'm tired, I'm weak, and I am so warm despite being in a drafty barn that creaks with every movement of the wind outside.

"Hey," I call out to Gia as I make my way toward her.

"Hello there. You slept a good long while. How you feeling?"

"Warm. Who'd have ever thought this old barn could be so warm right now." I look at Gia and she's very bundled up in her clothes. Oh, it isn't warm. "I have a fever running now, don't I?"

"Yes, and thanks for not being stubborn about admitting it."

"What next?"

"When first light comes, I'm going to have to go make a trip into town to find a way to dry out your clothes, restock some supplies, and figure out a plan. I'm hoping it won't take long, and I suspect that I'll find a town about five miles up the road."

"How can you guess that?" I ask.

"I peeked outside earlier from the window in the loft of the barn. I could see a faint glow coming from in the distance and it's a cloudy night. That leads me to believe…"

I interrupt. "…the lights lead to a town. Has anyone ever told you how brilliant you are?"

"Yes," Gia says. She's smiling at me. I think she's relieved that I'm awake, but still frightened because I am sick and not in a very ideal place for managing that.

"I'm glad that you're such a good doc. I'm guessing that I am going to need that."

"You'd better sit down. You look like you could topple over at any moment and quite honestly, I've had enough of lugging you around for quite some time. My entire body is aching from it."

I think hard and am trying to remember exactly what happened. It's fuzzy to me and I cannot really recall the details, but I know Gia did a lot. I remember the rope. "I'm very thankful to you for not letting this wanker just freeze to death in the creek."

"I'm not going to be the one to kill of the Rogue Spartan. You'll have to do that all on your own, Ben."

"Yah, about that…I was just being a jerk. I am not going to abandon everyone who trusts me and I'm sorry about being so stubborn about it all. It really caused some trouble, didn't it?"

"Indeed. Now, let's try to get a good night's rest so I can be ready to leave in the morning. I am going to trust that you won't be so daffy as to try and go anywhere in my absence."

"No worries here. Even if I were inclined, I'm not too comfortable running around bare naked outdoors in the middle of winter."

Gia laughs. I finally got her to relax with me. "Look Gia, I really am sorry," I say. I lean in and hug her. The wool of the blanket is so uncomfortable on my most private of parts and now they itch. I pull away, not wanting to itch my business in front of Gia. Gia laughs again, knowing just what the problem is.

It's time to sleep and morning comes and I find that I'm alone. I wonder what time it is and when Gia left.

Chapter Seventeen: January 3, 2043

I hear voices and I am panicked. Is it Gia? I can't be sure, but they are coming toward the barn and I am basically buck naked. I take the wool blanket off because my skin is starting to break out in a rash from it or whatever is on it. I look like a disaster—a spotted naked wild man, only not as buff as a Tarzan type guy and definitely not as tough as the first Spartans either.

The barn door swings open and I adjust my eyes to the light. I'm standing behind some old wooden crates, covering my lower half. My hand is over my eyes and I can see Gia's silhouette. Behind her at some big guys. I realize they are Fox and Pounder, and I can hear Felix, but don't see him. I can't believe it and I wonder how Gia did it. How did they get here so fast?

"Holy shit, RS. You look like crap," Felix calls out. He moves to the side of the guys so I can see him.

"Feeling like crap too."

"Well, we're here to get you out of this crap hole, and into a place that's a bit more conducive to getting better."

"You won't hear me complain. How'd you guys escape Chicago and how did you find us here?"

"Gia's very resourceful and knows how to take care of business. We'll just leave it at that." Felix says, not offering anything else. I wouldn't blame them if they didn't trust me anymore. I really fucked up when I tried to leave this place. I'll just have to work twice as hard to make it up and continue with the task of the Rogue Spartan.

Gia walks up to me and tosses me a duffle bag. "Here are your dried clothes and a few extra thermal layers to help regulate your body temperature until this fever passes."

"How do you know I…."

"Damn it, Ben. Don't argue with me. Put the shit on and let's get out of here." Gia is shooting out sparks from her eyes and it scares the hell out of me.

I decide to listen, like a little kid who just got scolded from his mother and is horrified. Well actually, the most horrifying part of it is the whooping laughter from Fox and Pounder. I'm very aware that Trapper isn't there and recall him falling from sight in Chicago.

"How many did we lose in Chicago?"

"Fifteen dead, thirty additional injured," Felix says.

"Everyone okay?"

"Everyone is still committed. The incident incited some unwelcomed riots, and now the Machine has placed a strict curfew on everything. No one is allowed outside accept for work, and to go to food lines on the day you're assigned to. It's madness, and worse yet—Redman likes it. This has helped him greatly."

"But it won't for long," I say, pulling my pants up. It feels great to have clothes on again and I am very thankful for it.

Gia is pulling something out of a small bag and I see that it's a needle. She turns to me. "Okay, we've got to give you a shot of some antibiotics. We don't have a week to have you down and out recovering from the *incident.* We've got to get to DC to take care of your little visit with Richards."

I look at Gia and whisper. "You told them about that?"

"Yes, we're a team and we don't keep secrets, Ben. This will help us get there and continue moving along at a quicker pace. On the way, Felix is going to stop and do a broadcast telling everyone a simple message."

"What?"

"That you live, Ben, and that Redman has motivated you to act more aggressively."

I smile. "That'll drive the egomaniac and the Redmanitized nuts."

"Fucking nuts," Gia adds.

We all take off walking across the field once again, clearly avoiding the route that I'd taken when I fell into the hidden creek. In the distance, by where the highway is, I can see a fairly large vehicle parked. It looks obvious and isn't very small or discreet. "Is that ours, guys?"

"Sure is," Fox says. "We have a series of vehicles lined up for the journey. With everyone of significance in the Machine after your ass a haul to the east coast is quite the task to arrange. We've done it though."

"That doesn't surprise me." I look at Fox and he is serious and focused. I mean, he always looks that way, but something about it is more intense now. I wonder if it's because of Trapper, but it doesn't feel like the right time to bring that up. Me taking care of what Trapper died trying to defend is what I can do to honor his name.

"Good, it shouldn't," Fox says.

It feels good to be moving in the vehicle and have a temporary sense of security before going to meet with Mr. Richards. I start to think about what I'm going to say once I'm actually there and what I'll do. I know it'll come to me and there's so much that I want to say to that dick. Words of seething vengeance seem childish now. I need the words that send a clear message and let him know that he's messing with the wrong guy. There will be consequences because of it. As we cross the boring miles I visualize the entire encounter as I stare out the window. I know that other people are talking, but I just don't wish to participate.

And the journey goes on.

Vehicle transfer in South Bend Indiana first.

Then Angola.

Next is Bowling Green.

And then on to Strongsville.

It seems like an eternity before the next transfer—Pittsburgh.

Cumberland is next.

Hagerland soon approaches.

And finally the destination of Washington DC is within twenty miles. It's almost time to do one of the most wildly insane and bold things I've ever done, and I am ready. I feel focused, my fever has broken, and Mr. Richards is going to be receiving a little visit from me. And if I'm not ready there's nothing else I can do…it is best just to believe I'm ready and know that Felix and company will not give me the okay to go in if I'm not. They've risked a lot and my death is not part of what is going to make their plan work.

Felix pulls into a gas station to do the expensive fill of the fuel tank. The Machine has made sure that every vehicle has a monitor on it to tell where and how far people are driving. This is how they determine the rate per gallon that you pay and monitor if you cross state lines that you shouldn't. All the stations are run by the EGA now and they can do a random inspection to make sure you're not skipping out on paying the Machine their fair share any time they want. Our current vehicle, the 2040 Solanoid Gastrofusion, is the only one that we've had to refill. The others had gone their intended distance without having to be filled. It seems like an odd error despite how meticulously everything has been planned.

The EGA monitor comes out and looks at all of us curiously. I am immediately disturbed by it, and keep looking out the window so I can hopefully keep my back to him. I hear Felix talking to him a mile a minute, using his flamboyant personality to distract the guy. Is it working? I have no clue, but I sure as hell hope so.

I hear the monitor ask, "Can I see your cross line registration?"

"Sure, let's go inside and get out of this wind. I'll pay up and show the registration," Felix says.

"Okay," the monitor responds.

I cannot help but turn my head and watch them walk into the station's door. How is Felix going to get through this? Maybe he's going to pay him off. I soon find out the answer and it definitely is not what I expected.

Felix opens the door for the guy and then slams it shut, using a small metal bar that was in his coat pocket to jam the door. He slides it into the handle and blocks the entrance. The guy turns around and knows what's happening immediately. I see him reach for his communicator and stare at Felix.

Felix runs and pulls out a gun, shooting all the cameras in range with masterful precision. Will that stop them from looking at the digital images that go right to the EGA though? It won't. Why is he doing this? It's never going to work.

Just seconds later Felix is in the car and we are driving off quickly. "Close call, wouldn't you say?" Trapper asks.

"That prick wouldn't let up. Had no choice. Now, let's get out of here, eat a bit, and make our way to Richards's apartment building full speed ahead." Felix floors it and smiles, acting like nothing just happened.

Gia and Fox are quiet, just like me know. I know my heart rate has begun to accelerate to a level that is anything besides composed. Damn it. Why did he do that? I realize that I still haven't said shit, but I keep turning around fully expecting to see the sirens on the massive MCU highway rovers coming toward us. There is nothing.

Finally I break my silence. "Felix, how did you pull that off? Aren't you on the digitals at the EGA?"

"Yes, but we'll be fine. You've got to have faith, RS."

"I thought you would just pay him off or something like that."

"That guy is a known climber and there is no way he'd take a pay-off if he thought he could bust someone— you—and reach the upper ranks of management of the EGA."

"He knew it was me?"

"You're still not grasping just how infamous you've become, RS. I guess that makes sense since most of your work thus far has been done in isolation." Felix takes his hands off the wheel and puts them up in the air, gesturing that he doesn't get my questioning.

"So, is everything in place for after DC to start the other initiatives to overturn the Machine?" I ask this, realizing that time has run out. I'm getting my last wish of meeting with Richards, but very soon everything will be beyond him. I'll be actually pursuing ways to infiltrate the Machine and get to Redman himself.

"It is. In fact, I am coordinating everything so that after Richards we should be able to have a little meeting with Redman and scare the crap out of that coward until he begs us for his life in exchange for whatever we want from the Machine."

"We wouldn't take a deal, would we?" I ask. Something about Felix's tone bothers me. Why would we go through all of this and compromise with the Machine. We're the Anti-Machine.

"Hell no, but when they beg you know you have them where you want them."

Gia turns to me and I realize she's been equally as quiet as me. "It's nice to have you back and to know that you believe."

I wink at her, knowing that I can't do what just popped into my mind. Our time will come eventually. *If you go at your pace it may be when you're forty.*

I notice Felix staring at me in the mirror. He has a shit ass grin on his face and I'm busted. He saw me wink and my little bit of inspiration to lighten my mood and calm my nerves turns to a red prickly rash traveling up the back of my neck. Or maybe it's the excitement of feeling Gia's muscular leg rub up against mine.

It's time to change the subject. "Do you know where Richards' apartment is?" I am talking to no one in particular.

"Naturally," Felix responds. "He is living in the penthouse apartment of the Redman Cabinet Sanctuary Building. It's a big shiny monument to the higher ups that is heavily guarded, and full of the most advanced security systems ever."

"Advanced?" I ask.

"Yep, lasers that'll chop your knee caps off if you cross them and are unaware."

"Great," I say. I decide to stop asking questions for right now. I have to get into the building and there must be a weakness. It's an old lesson that I've learned about the Machine from hacking. Everything they create has some weakness because of their arrogance. They may not want to admit they are human, but they are as weak a human as one could be.

We pull up to a parking lot just before curfew and go in, taking a reserved spot. I don't bother to ask if it is Felix's because truthfully it doesn't matter. I am here and I am ready.

Chapter Eighteen: January 10, 2043

I'm in luck. There's a dumpster that is big enough for me to hide behind. Hopefully someone comes out the door before too long. It's night time, and there should be custodians cleaning the common areas of the apartment…I think.

Next to me I find a metal pipe and I pick it up. Can I use this if I need to? I think I can, mostly because I don't have a choice. I have a small laser gun, the LDR147, but am not really that trained in using it. I'm also carrying my laser jammer just in case, and hope that I don't need to test it in real time. It was enough for me to see that it could work when I left the bunker.

This is what I know about the Redman Cabinet Sanctuary Building:

- The MCU patrol it heavily and have a mini station set up right inside of it.
- There are fourteen floors of homes, with the most protected people being on the top floors. Naturally, Richards is on the 13th floor, with the 14th floor being reserved for private soirees that Redman likes to hold on occasion.
- Its security system is crazy, but not inaccessible. Everyone who works there has the highest level of clearance in the Machine regardless of their job. Most of the maintenance people are relatives of those who live there too, making them more trustworthy in the eyes of the Government.
- From the time of entry I have exactly thirty minutes to do what I must and then I'll have to get out or else Felix, Gia, and the others will take off. I'll have to make my way to our safe spot by foot.

This is what I know about me:

- I am one guy with a big ass task right now.
- I want to talk to Richards and see what he has to say.

- I am feeling confident.
- I know that I cannot hesitate under any circumstances when I do this.

A long time passes by with nothing. I look down at my watch and see that I've been there an hour, but it feels like two. My legs are cramping from hunching over and I stand up to stretch. I pause. There is someone talking on the other side of the thick steel door. I'm surprised I can hear them, but I can. I hope it's just one person because I don't know if I can handle two.

The person is still talking and their hand is pressing down on the bar that will open the back door. I can see a small crack of light and know that I could go and swing that door open. It would definitely surprise the guy, but I don't think the time is right. I'd like him to come outside or at least further out.

Finally, I hear the guy say he'll see the other guy later at break time. The door swings open and I am standing against the brick portion of the wall, blending into the darkness. The lights that flood the area are somewhat scattered, making it easy for me to find the shadow I'm standing in.

The guy turns toward me, making his way with a bag of garbage to put in the dumpster. I take the pipe and swing it into his stomach with all the force I can muster. He gasps and leans over. I have no choice and now I smack him on the head too. He drops down, out cold, and I throw his garbage bag into the dumpster and then find the keys on him. It's a scan card and also physical keys. I really don't know what I need, but I take it all. In an effort that takes all my muscles I pick the guy up and slump him into the dumpster too so he isn't just laying in the alley. I shut the lid and put a piece of wood through the latch so he can't open it up if he wakes up.

I place the scan card into the slot, and hear a series of beeps. The lock unlatches and I slowly swing the door open, looking around before I enter. There are stairs going up and down, and a hallway that goes to the left. I know I need to make my way to the thirteenth floor so I decide to take the stairs that go up.

My footsteps create a soft echo in the sterile stairwell and I am walking as slowly as I can so I am not too loud. I know that I don't have much time, but I feel like running will be a bad thing...cause me to miss something.

Now I am up to the 10th floor and I cannot believe how stark white and bright the stairwell is. It almost hurts my eyes and I wish I had some glasses to wear. The door from the hallway on the 10th floor swings open and I am standing behind it. I don't know who is there and I pull out my laser gun. I don't hear voices so I assume they are alone. I breathe in and point the gun right at a guy. I watch him turn around and quickly assess that he's not much bigger than me. His eyes widen as he looks at me and then the gun and I notice a communicator on his belt. I have no time to spare. I pull the trigger, sending a laser blast into his side. It's enough to hurt him, but hopefully not kill him.

He grabs his side and looks down. He's in shock and cannot believe what just happened. Shit, I can't believe what I just did. It is necessary though. Now the bright white stairwell has spatters of dark red blood spattered all over it. I lean over and grab the communicator from the guy's belt and his keys. I will just have to leave him there.

Now I know I'm treading on even more dangerous grounds and that I have to move quickly. There's no other option. I bolt up to the thirteenth floor and find the key to open it up. I enter the corridor and see three hallways, each with a door at the end. I run to one and I see the name Marietta. I know he's a cabinet member for Redman. I charge to another door and find the name I am hoping to see—Richards.

I see a scan hole by the door and am not sure if the cards I have will work. I decide to try because fumbling with keys and keyholes would be too challenging. I swipe the card and a digital message displays itself. It reads, *enter code*. Code? Damn, I don't know what the code is. I drop the other scan card as I try to scramble, thinking of what the code might be. I happen to look down and see a six digit code written in marker on the back side of the card on the floor. Could that be it?

With great care I punch in 52-37-36-2-85-20. I sigh and press enter. Unbelievable! I hear the latch release and I slowly walk into the apartment. Lights are on and I hear music coming from a different room.

As my eyes scan the place and my ears try to tune in to the location where Richards may be I cannot help but admire how beautiful the place is. Nothing is spared on Cabinet members and VPs apparently. Where others have modest living accommodations, these people have the best of the best. Everything looks expensive and I'm not expert in decorating, but I am positive that these fixtures are every bit as expensive as they look.

Unlike the hallways and stairwell, the ambiance in the apartment is amazing. It has good lighting that is soft and doesn't make your eyeballs sting from the glare.

"I was wondering when I'd be seeing you, Ben."

I jump. I peer toward a corner and can see the silhouette of a man there. I know the voice well enough…it's Richards.

"How did you know I'd come?"

"I'm guessing you want answers, and you're likely a bit pissed off at me."

"Why me?"

"Why you? Out of all questions you have, that's what you choose to start with." Richards walks over into the light and is looking at me. He is calm and composed, not even startled by my presence. From what he just said I can only assume he is expecting me. "You have been the one that I've been waiting for a good long while. I first spotted you back at school, and have planned every step of your career and skills along the way."

"You're full of shit. You didn't know what I'd do after you...you..."

"Killed your friends," Richards finishes for me.

I feel angry, but I know that I must be calm. "They didn't have to die."

"Yes, they did. They were not working with you, Ben. You don't realize what a favor I did. They were against you."

"That's a lie."

"Is it? Well, it's certainly not my spot to convince you, but from what I've seen you are a fairly intelligent guy. What is it they call you know? The Rogue Spartan."

I don't want to respond right away. I feel like Richards is trying to trip me up and I don't know what he'll attempt to do. In an effort to protect myself I put my hand on the laser gun, hoping it will show that I am not afraid to use it if I must.

"Ah, getting a taste for killing people, Ben? You were rather kind to the guy the stairwell, but I'm afraid he wasn't so kind in return after he was found."

How does he know about that? I don't like this. There's no secrecy or element of surprise. Something's wrong. "Not all of us are egotistical asses like you are."

"Egotistical yes, but I dare say you are too. You've suddenly realized that you have certain skills and now you're ready to make a real difference. Little Ben has grown up. Don't worry though. I don't hold that against you. I have something to tell you that I believe you'll like and   appreciate."

"What?" I cannot help but be curious about his statement.

"Surely you've wondered why you, someone who has no proven past abilities, has been able to elude the MCU and my special field agents rather simply."

I know he's right and I don't want to admit it to him. "You've underestimated me, nothing more."

"Well, I have underestimated you somewhat. I will give you that, Ben. However, everything that has come your way and all the steps that you've done have been under my direction—no one else's. They may have appeared to be your ideas, but they were definitely planted there by me."

"What do you mean?"

"Well, think about your best source that you've come across since that day when we paid you and your friends a little visit. It's been Felix, correct?"

"Correct," I say. So he knows Felix. That really is not surprising though because Felix is a rather notable figure.

"Why don't we sit down and have a drink. I'll explain everything to you. You can set your gun down, as I know you aren't going to shoot me and I have no intentions of shooting you. I've taken you too far on this journey to quit and start over with someone else."

I do take a seat. My legs feel numb and I cannot figure out what's going on. "Okay then, tell me what's happening."

Mr. Richards hands me a drink and I am glad to take it. I recognize the taste—it is bourbon and just as good as the bourbon that gave me that throbbing hangover back at the bunker.

"Ben, we are more alike than what you thought. I, just like you, do not wish to live in a world where Redman is the self proclaimed leader of our country. The man is a fool."

"Then why have you worked so hard to make your way up to the VP spot?"

"Good question. Every person you investigated and I eliminated from power was a move to slowly infiltrate Redman's cabinet with people who truly were opposed to him. He's clueless about it."

"That's a big plan. Why share it with me?"

"Because I need the Rogue Spartan to keep scaring and distracting Redman. He is terrified of the people rising up against him—it's safe to say that is his single biggest fear."

"What do you see happening after Redman is no longer in power?"

"I see a new President, one with a greater vision and ability to connect with the American people coming into power."

"You?" I ask this with sincere curiosity.

"If the people would want me I would consider it, but no—me being in power is not a driving force to this decision. You may think that I'm a kiss ass to Redman, as well as the other higher ups, but we all have interests to protect too. Never forget that."

"So, what's next?" I know that I'm running out of time and that Felix is about to leave the spot in the parking lot.

"Next is us coordinating a way for you to keep doing what you've been doing without getting killed by Redman's orders to do so. Then you will have to go and kill him when the time is right."

"When is the time right?"

"Ben, the time is right on a very special day, a symbolic day if you will—July 4."

"That's still a lot of months away."

"That's okay. Your skills will only improve, and you will also have time to solidify your base of committed members to the Anti-Machine. Six months is nothing compared to the overall picture. You must be patient."

"I'll do it, but when that time comes I want my friend Cal to be released from ITC custody and be freed in exchange."

"A small request and one that I am sure I can manage."

"I won't kill anyone until I see he is safe."

"Okay, I believe you. Your loyalty to your friends is considerably more impressive than theirs to you."

"Why do you keep talking that way?"

"No reason. I must say that it is a rare quality to find such dedication. It's actually part of the reason that you were my choice for the past five years now. It was no easy task finding someone to carry on Dr. Secton's infamous mission."

I pause. It seems odd thinking of Richards as respecting Secton. They seem the opposite in every way. "How will I communicate with you when July 4 nears?"

"I'll give you a number. It goes directly to me and it's a private line. You contact me on July 3, and I'll give you specifics on how to enter into Camp Redman, where the President will be entertaining all us cabinet members and a select few dignitaries from across the globe. Make sure you're near the camp then, okay?"

"I can do that. Well, this has been...interesting. I must go now so if you'll excuse me."

"Most certainly. I look forward to a mutually beneficial relationship in the upcoming months, Ben."

"Who can I tell about this?"

"Well, I suppose you must tell your small group of people. They are likely able to tell that something's going on, and your new agenda may conflict with the one they wish you to follow."

"So, they are not partnered up with you?"

"No, they are not," Richards tells me. This is good to hear because a part of me is wondering if I have been played for an idiot by Felix, Fox, Pounder, and worse of all…Gia.

"How do you know they won't want to get you? They hate the Machine and everything it represents, you know?"

"I am trusting in your skills and influence to ensure my safety. That's the only way this will work, you know. We must trust."

I don't say another word. There's nothing left to say.

Chapter Nineteen: January 11, 2043
I am at the Larkman Cottage just outside of Baltimore and I'm guessing that it's about a hundred years old. It's drafty and definitely reminiscent of a time before the authoritarian industrial revolution. I took the Greyhound here and am glad to have had a very uneventful trip. There is so much to process about my entire encounter with Richards, the plan for Redman, and how I am going to tell Felix, Gia, Fox, and Pounder. Truthfully, I'm clueless as to what any of them will say.

"Good work getting into the Sanctuary and getting out alive." Felix slaps me on the back, goes over to sit back in a leather chair, and crosses his one leg over the other. He's staring at me and I can see just how curious he is to hear my story. Gia is standing in the corner, while Fox and Pounder are leaning against the entrance to the cozy living room of the cottage.

"It was quite the experience," I say.

"So what happened then?" Gia asks. She sounds anxious and I look at her. She looks calm, but her voice doesn't seem that way.

"Well Gia, remember when I told you that everything had seemed like it was too easy for me at times?" Gia nods yes. "I was right. It has been. Apparently Redman wants me to succeed and has been helping up to this point and is interested in ensuring my success."

"Why?" Felix asks.

"He says he is trying to get rid of Redman, doesn't want him in power because he's a bad leader."

"That's an understatement," Fox says.

"And let me guess…he wants to help," Felix says.

"Yah. It caught me off guard though, and I don't feel like I can trust him. I guess if he gets me in to do what must be done with Redman I can't complain. Any help from within is beneficial."

"When does he want you to do it?" Felix asks.

"July 4."

"That's a bloody long ways away," Gia says and I nod, knowing I had the same concern. "And what are you supposed to do until then? It seems like a waste of six months."

"Build up the Anti-Machine movement further and keep getting under Redman's skin."

"Do you trust Richards?" Felix asks. That is the big question and I don't answer right away. It would be a lie to say I trust him completely. After all, I've wished ill upon the man for a rather long time now. However, if he is a valuable asset to help in bringing down the Machine I would be dumb not to take advantage of that.

"I don't know that I trust him, but I am willing to take my chances for using his help to get to Redman when the time is right."

"You think the 4th is symbolic?" Felix is leaning forward now, trying to assess my reactions. It's making me uncomfortable.

"That's what he said." I stare at him, not willing to turn away. I wonder if he thinks that Richards is going to rain on his parade. I know that I'm the figurehead, but suspect that Felix believes he's the leader. I need him, but I question if he's the leader of this movement. I'll give him the inspiration factor though.

"What about communication?"

"He gave me this number," I say and pull out the piece of paper. "I'm supposed to give him a call on July 3 and make sure that we're all prepared and near Camp Redman. He'll have all the details ready then."

"And he okayed you telling us?" Fox asks.

"He said he knew that you were a part of what would keep me moving forward and spreading the message. He didn't mind."

"Any other details?" Felix continues.

I replay the conversation and remember one—a very important one. "He's agreed to get Cal released." Felix looks at me oddly and his expression lightens.

"Good call for you, Ben. Well, I guess you've decided on it so it's settled then. It's time to track down a new place for a broadcasted message, and go into some fucking intensive training to make sure you've got the chutzpah it'll take to address this when the time comes. Mother-fuckin-fire-works-are-going-to-fly!" Felix jumps up and just like that he seems satisfied. He isn't one to dwell, I'll give him that.

Chapter Twenty: April 4, 2043

I'm exhausted and impatient from waiting. It's been almost three months and I've been working my ass off— we all have been. Physically, I'm getting better and emotionally I am feeling like I can do this. It doesn't feel like I'm selling myself on what I can do anymore. I've finally accepted it as my reality and it's made a big difference.

My new level of confidence is helping me out a lot with something that I've determined that I really want and am going to pursue. It's Gia. At times I think it may be that she's a sexy distraction from all the intensity of the Anti-Machine movement and the increasing demands of my time. Then I stand back, observe her in action, and just know that she's the one.

Our new temporary home of Larkman Cottage is a cozy place. Felix comes and goes on occasion, working with people everywhere and converting them over to the Anti-Machine movement. The rest of us stay here and now Gia and I are sharing a room too. I don't mind saying that the sharing has extended a bit further and she is teaching me some physical moves that are blowing my mind and making other parts erupt too. It's unbelievable.

The most exciting conversions to our side are getting to the ones closest to Redman—the MCU that protects him. We've had some great fortune and it is getting us closer to where we need to be. Felix says he did that, but I can't help but speculate that Richards actually did. After all, he is the one slowly converting the inner workings of the Cabinet to people who oppose Redman. Sometimes I wonder if they know what they even stand for. They seem to be easily swayed by the promise of something better, but not really willing to put themselves out there to get it. I've put myself out there and now I have expectations for those who want to help me to do the same.

Today is field training and target practice. I am better than when I started, but still have an average shot at best. My only goal is to be equal to the true marksmen—Fox, Pounder, and Gia. If I can match them I'll be sitting good.

"With this exercise you are going to have to make sure you shoot the guys who are out to blast your ass, RS," Fox says.

"How do I identify them? All the targets look to be in street clothes."

"It'll take a quick assessment of weapon type, personality evaluation, and also their shoes."

"Their shoes?"

"All Machine protectors wear Government issued boots."

"What happens if I shoot a friendly dummy?"

"It'll start on fire, and that'll let you know—and all of us—that you messed up. Let me just say that we are all hoping that doesn't happen because if we're going to be backing you for this mission we don't really want you to be the one who does us in if we get our heads blasted off."

"Got it."

"Oh, and one other thing."

"What?" I ask. If nothing else, I know that one other thing is usually something major.

"We'll have fake lasers rifles and be in the woods shooting at you too. Don't let us get you."

"And how do I stop you?"

"You just do. Naturally you have a simulated laser too because we are not about to risk you actually getting that ace shot in this drill." Pounder says. It's a rare moment where he speaks and certainly no secret that he's quieter than Fox and Gia.

I have to put a blindfold on until I hear a shot ring out. I am standing on the edge of the woods, feeling the energy surging through my body with the drill. I have learned enough that I should be able to be fairly responsive, and knowing that I could get tagged by someone added to the intensity of the drill.

The shot rings out and I whip the blindfold off and start walking into the woods. It is mid morning and there are shadowed parts in the forest that are great hiding places. Trying to spot them is a bit interesting and on occasion my eyes play tricks on me. I fire at an old stump that just happens to look like a person's silhouette. After I realize what I'd done I hope no one has seen me.

I can hear my boots crunching lightly on the sticks in the woods. The ground is damp because it is early spring and there has been excessive melt-off from the thick snow that had covered the ground during the winter.

Through the corner of my eye I sense something moving. I put my finger on the trigger and whip my head to the side, hoping to see what it is quickly and assess it equally quick. I smile. I see a mannequin standing there, dressed in casual clothes and a leather jacket. But damn…I can't see the boots. I start to walk toward the mannequin slowly, hoping to get a glimpse of them. I am stealth like and I am mad. I see a red laser come through a thicket of bushes and it land itself squarely on my chest.

"Got you," Gia yells. I hear her laughter.

Ignoring Gia's comment, I decide to come back to that mannequin later and go off to the right. Mentally I have to forget about Gia getting me and get back in the game. Focus is essential. I notice another body shape hiding behind a tree. It is very still and I am unsure if it is a person or a dummy. I veer to the right and walk around until I can get a visual from a different angle in the distance. It is indeed a dummy and I look down and see the thick heeled black boots with the red stripe around their sole. It is a Machine dummy.

I pick up my laser gun and look through the scope, aligning the heart of the dummy with the line of the laser. I shoot and am excited to see the dummy fall down—no fire. A sound whizzes over my head at the same time and I turn, seeing another dummy there and instinctually fire. It blazes up and I growl, irritated with myself. I am panicked and as a result I allowed my adrenaline to rule my judgment.

The exercise continues on for two more hours and I am exhausted. It's mentally taxing even though I know that no one can really die. I can't stand it and I wonder how soldiers get the mentality to deal with this type of intensity. It's hard, it's challenging, and I have a new admiration for the mindset of people who can be successful with combative exercises. I'm very aware of my subconscious shouting out that I hopefully can get Redman to surrender peacefully. Yes, you can say I'm a dreamer, but I don't care. Some pretty great things have started with a dream in the past, and even the Machine cannot steal dreams—even ones meant to stifle them.

By the end of the exercise I accidentally get two friendly dummies with my laser fire and as a result they start on fire. However, I do get all of the Machine's dummies and in the kill zone with my first shot. This makes me happy. Better yet, Gia is the only one who was able to get me and I learned from that. It prepared me. Overall, I've done better than I have ever done and I consider it a mild victory.

Night time finally arrives and I'm exhausted, but happy. We are all sitting around the kitchen table, laughing and talking about the day's drill.

"You're getting better," Fox says to me.

"Thanks. I still have a ways to go, but I think I'll have it down by the time we head to DC. It's still three months away."

We continue to talk and are surprised to see Felix show up. It's not that we ever know when to expect him, but he was just here the week before and usually doesn't make it back that quickly.

"I have excellent news that I wanted to personally share."

"What's that?" I ask, not having any idea of what it may be.

"Our membership has grown. We now have large units in every continental state and rumor has it that Alaska has a strong unit there just in case. They're naturally off the grid so they are lucky bastards up there. Hawaii is even showing signs of the Anti-Machine as of late and that is just about the same as China turning into a democracy."

"Any idea on new numbers then?" Gia asks.

"Get this—estimates show that we may have upwards of one million that are actively involved, and an additional three million that help in small ways but don't actively participate."

"Holy shit," I say. I cannot believe how much support that many people bring the cause. This is really happening and the Rogue Spartan is set to go.

"Should we do a broadcast?"

"You must be reading my mind RS," Felix says.

We drive into town and sneak in through the back door of a television station control center that has someone who is sympathetic to the Rogue Spartan doing security. He knows it is going to happen and we tie him up and blindfold him. He must be protected because there are little spy cam's everywhere that the Machine plants into its stations. It is part of their intimidation techniques because no one can tell when the cameras are on and that implies that the workers in these places will always do what is right by the Machine in order to protect them.

I am excited and I begin. It's going to be short, sweet, and to the point.

It's been three months since we spoke last fellow Spartans and I am excited to tell you that our numbers are growing every day. I'm very comfortable letting you all know that our numbers are greater than the Machine's and they are scared.

More people are coming forth to help us with our cause and this summer fireworks are going to fly. Everything will be different and it will be our time to shine again. That is when we will restore our constitution.

For now, think wisely, be safe, and don't collapse under the fear and tyranny of the Machine. We are greater than Redman as individuals and as a group we are greater than anything the Machine can throw at us.

Be well and remember that prosperity is on the horizon.

Chapter Twenty-One: July 4, 2043

Knowing what is about to happen today is hard to process despite my planning for it. Me and an small army of about one hundred militia are going to go and approach Redman. It's time for action and there is nothing that will stand in my way. The call I made to Richards yesterday provided many details and it has solved the remainder of the missing links of the plan.

It's an intricate network of people that are helping Felix, Gia, Pounder, Fox, and I get into Camp Redman, the same place that used to be the presidential retreat known as Camp David. Like all other things that symbolized American history, Redman thought it best that he rewrite history to reflect him and his accomplishments. I always thought the appropriate title of that book should be, How One Jackass Ruined America. That seems fitting, but he is more likely to name it something like, President Redman…Saint and Scholar.

This camp is where all of the top security equipment exists for the United States now, along with an arsenal of weapons that could easily wipe out anyone who tried to invade the premises or harm the president. It's another one of those obsessive security measures that the Machine deems brilliant, but it won't work. My militia guys are used to living off the grid and they know how to get most anywhere unnoticed. Many of them come from the proud traditions of elite sniper troops, Army Rangers, and Navy Seals. Redman may have eliminated those positions due to fear of retaliation, but their methods and histories have been carried down from one generation to the next.

We'll have to travel by foot for a good many miles in order to reach the outskirts of Camp Redman in order to ensure none of our vehicles are spotted. It's a taxing hike through the forests and jagged bits of rocks that have tumbled from the mountains that surround the presidential compound. One of our guys has already rolled his ankle, making him ineffective. He's one of our best shooter's too. We'll keep him camouflaged in a tree though and armed in case he needs to fire to protect one of us upon exist. It's all yet to be determined and the best we can hope to do is prepare for every possible scenario to some extent. Perfection is impossible.

I'll give it to Richards…the guy thinks of everything. Through Felix and the news we've found out that the entire cabinet is at the compound today for a 4th of July celebration of sorts. The bastards are probably celebrating how fast they ruined a country with unlimited potential, flawed as it may be at times.

Knowing that there are MCU that patrol the woods at all times when the President is at the compound makes for a very dull hike. We cannot talk and must keep our ears alert to anything that may be happening. Felix is carrying a high powered microphone, designed to pick up voices or footsteps from great distances. It's an incredible device and a prototype of the MCU. How he got it is a mystery and I don't think I want to know. Gia asked him though and he only smiled at her with that shit ass grin.

Fox is out in front of me, charged with being my bodyguard if you will. I should mind, but I don't. Why would I? The guy is a beast and highly capable. He's trained me good, but I'm not him yet. Suddenly Fox puts his arm out, signaling for me to stop. I come to an abrupt halt and try to listen. I don't hear anything and I look over to Fox, seeing if I can tell what he may have noticed.

He's scanning the area in front of us, as if he's looking for something in particular. I can't notice anything of distinction, but he is frowning. I watch him pick his laser rifle up and point toward the trees. Without warning he fires off the laser, which is unlike guns of old because it's silent. No one can hear it go off; however we quickly hear the scream of a man falling out of the tree and down to the ground. He has a uniform on, but it's not MCU— it's like the uniforms of the guys that Richards had sent to Cal's apartment that day over a year ago. I still don't have clear answers as to who these guys are and it would be good to know. Are they worse than MCU or just a group of people promoting their own agenda? Yah, I know that I am doing that same thing, but I can say with all certainty that I don't have any illusions of being the president or anyone who goes through life casting out power play after power play. I just want to restore what once was to the best it can be and enjoy some of the freedom that I've only heard about, never having the chance to experience.

I lean in to Fox's ear and whisper, "Are there going to be more?"

He doesn't answer me, just shaking his head no. He looks confident and I don't have a clue how he can determine that from what just happened. Maybe the guy was meant to distract.

We've reached the point in the woods where we'll be splitting up into three groups. Felix will be leading one, Fox and I another, and Gia and Pounder the third. This is how we are going to have access to the three sides of Camp Redman that are accessible via the woods. The other side isn't accessible due to the huge mountain you'd have to climb and its lack of timber upon its side. It would be easy to be spotted.

It's a bit ridiculous for me to be thinking of this now, being in the middle of a day unlike any other I'll ever have again, but I feel nervous not having Gia in my group. She's highly capable of taking care of herself, but I just feel anxious not having her near me. I smile, thinking of what she'd say to that thought as I walk along.

We are all wearing black clothes, black stocking hats, black waterproof and laser proof kevaline protected boots, thin black gloves that hide fingerprints and allow for full uninterrupted hand function for this mission. Our faces also have a sheer spray-on black paint on them and mine is itching me badly. It's not suppose to have negative effects on anyone's skin, but it's driving me crazy. I have no clue if its bugging others the same way because we can't talk.

There's about one mile left for me to go before I get to the south side of Camp Redman and prepare to enter the compound. I cannot stop the movies going on in my mind of how this is going to play out today. I feel confident, but I am very aware of just how much is riding on this day. It's not about me either; it's about all of the others that are sacrificing so much because they believe in me, the Rogue Spartan.

Cal is also on my mind. I know he's in the compound somewhere and I'm so excited that I can help him get out of custody from the ITC. Of course, I cannot guarantee that we'll make it out alive, but anything has to be better than being one of their captives, right?

We reach a small clearing at the edge of the woods and can see MCU walking around in the distance, looking bored as they patrol. It's not very hot in this part of the country, even in July, but they all look miserable in their thick heavy uniforms, lugging around their big laser guns, LRG-43a's from the looks of it. A blast from one of those guns could blow a hole in the side of a building, or disintegrate a section of this forest and whatever happens to be in that area.

In the distance I can hear a bird calling out. I'm not sure what type of bird it is because it's only been a handful of times that I've ever heard a real bird before. They tend to not want to hang out in New York City, and well...aside from this past year I've always hung out in New York City.

Fox has his binoculars up to his face and is looking for the other two parts of our group by the areas they are supposed to be at. Felix is taking the east side and he should have already arrived. Gia and Pounder are making their way to the west side and that's where they are to remain, serving as protection if we need to abort the plan and flee.

Fox points over to the east and mouths, "Felix is over there." I nod, looking in that direction. I hear the bird noise again, but this time I have a feeling that it is the MCU guy. All the other guys patrolling seem to not notice what's going on and I am not sure if they're clueless or choosing to not see what's going on. I find out quickly that they are casually turning their back to the locations where we are to the south and Felix's team is.

I see Felix and a group quickly run to the compound. There are no windows on the side they are facing and I look straight ahead. The south side of the place has giant windows everywhere and I wonder how I'll get in without any problems.

About ten minutes pass and Felix shows himself from a door that is facing our direct, whistling out. Fox stands up and the rest of us follow suit. We make a mad sprint across the lawn and I am relieved to see that the MCU are not really into their job for Redman, preferring to help us out. That is some connection and one that I never would have thought I could rely on from past experiences.

Now there are sixty of us inside and it's time to go crazy. I need to get to Redman in order to carry out the quest of the Rogue Spartan—that's my primary objective. Fox is there to help cover me and give me an extra set of eyes.

Felix…well, I know he's set this all up, but I'm not really sure why he's there because he doesn't have a specific part of the plan to carry out. Still, there's safety in numbers and I can trust these people. *Can I trust myself?*

We are in Camp Redman and like so many things this past year I am a bit thrown off by how easy it has been to get in. I'm all for great planning, but when things look easy they are often full of glitches and surprises. My grandpa had taught me that when I was a little boy and I have always remembered it.

Although we're inside the compound, we are all very quiet still, not wanting to alert anyone to the fact that we're there. Our plan is based on surprise. I do wonder how Richards has kept Cal hidden for this though or explained his presence. Well, he's a manipulative guy and can certainly think of a lie just about as easy as he can breath, I'd imagine.

Felix comes up to me and whispers, "You and I are going to go up to find Redman solo. Come on?"

"I thought Fox was suppose to be with me," I whisper back, not sure why Felix is suddenly adjusting the plan.

"He'll protect you easier down here. My source has just told me that Redman is in the security room."

"Where all the computer systems are based?"

"Yes."

"Let's go," I say and an MCU that's standing at the end of the long hallway of the door we entered into points to the right, indicating we should go that way. I cannot help but ask Felix if he's sure we're not being set up.

"I can assure you that we are not being set up."

Ten minutes later we have gone down a black flight of stairs and are in the basement bunker area of Camp Redman, preparing to enter the room that controls most everything that happens in the whole damn country. *Holy fuck*, I think. I can feel a rush going through my body. It's a bit easier to put into perspective how assholes can get power rushes when they have access to this type of technology.

Chapter Twenty-Two: July 4, 2043 at 2 p.m.
I am standing there with Felix and we breathe in deeply. It's time to approach the man that I've been bugging for the past year and encourage him to step down. Of course, encouragement is a loose term because he doesn't have a choice and in a few minutes his acts against the constitution are going to stop and he can choose if he wants to rot in one of his prison camps or die. He's been so ruthless to so many people that the innocent in those camps would probably make sure he met a terrible fate anyways. I know it's wrong of me to smile as I think of him being tormented and begging for mercy, but he needs

to understand how so many people felt doing the same things because of his ruthless actions.

"I'll stand out here for a bit while you go in," Felix says.

"How many people do you think are in there?" I whisper.

"Five max and a few of them aren't going to stop you. You'll have to be quick enough to figure out which ones you need to stop as soon as you enter into that door."

"You couldn't have told me that sooner?"

"You would have freaked RS. You've been training for this. You'll be fine," Felix replies. "I'm putting the code in now."

Felix pulls out a piece of paper and enters in the code to get to the building. It's the one that I gave him yesterday after my conversation with Richards and he had insisted on holding on it. I didn't know why yesterday, but today I do. He obviously wants to be here and knew it all along, but chose not to share it.

The code is entered into the door and it opens up. I'm surprised that it seems more challenging to break into TerraCorp than it does to break into this place. No eye scan. No voice recognition. At first no one looks at me immediately and that's a good thing because I can assess who I may need to fire at and who may wish to fire at me. The laser jammer is at my side and I'm hoping that it works. It's still iffy and certainly could have been built better, but I did the best I could with what I had.

One guy turns around abruptly and looks at me, trying to determine what the deal is. After all, I'm all in black. It's only brief though and he turns back around. My side.

I take a step forward and can hear the familiar voice of President Redman although I cannot see him. My movement captures someone else's attention and they quickly turn around, immediately lifting up their weapon to fire at me. I beat them to it and fire first with the gun in my right hand while pressing the laser jammer with my right. Their laser bolt refracts and cracks the glass window that protects the computers in the distance from particles in the air and temperature variations.

Now everyone is focused on me and I know that I have one man down and there are three more staring at me. I am looking at them and everyone seems unsure of what to do and is trying to assess the situation. Redman comes flying around the corner and pauses too. He's staring at me and doesn't know what to think. He looked around at the other men. "Intruder…shoot him NOW!" he orders.

One guy turns toward Redman and lifts his gun. For a second I think he's going to shoot him, but he quickly turns the weapon in a different direction and fires off two quick blasts that go right through the heart of the two other men. Okay. My side. Now things are about to get interesting.

"President Redman, it's so nice to see you," I say.

"Who are you?" Redman asks, glaring in my direction. I can almost hear the wheels in his head turning as he tries to assess this situation and find a way to talk himself out of being harmed in any possible way.

"I do apologize for the dark appearance, but I'm most sure you would recognize me if I took off the make-up."

"Wait…that voice. It's familiar. Are you him?"

"Him?" I ask, feigning genuine confusion.

"The prick who has been trying to sabotage me?"

"Sabotage…now that's a very harsh way to put it. By you thinking that you are above all others you' have certainly sabotaged yourself. I'm excited to let you know that you're reign of terror is over and we'll be making a few changes in the United States."

"You can't stop me from doing shit, boy," Redman says, suddenly showing his fire.

"I've been quite the nuisance for you for the past year now. I suspect that with those that are rallying behind me we can do quite a bit of "shit", as you put it."

"Cowards hiding behind the scenes. You don't know what it takes to run a country and how many people don't have the ability to make a god damn decision on their own."

"They used to know how until you authoritarian loving propagandists told them they were too ignorant. How long has this plan to strip people's freedoms away until they no longer knew what they were existed?"

"Man didn't me to do anything to take that away. They were all too damn lazy to fight for their freedoms. That's not my fault. I haven't been lazy, and I assure you that I have worked my ass off for everything I have. I've earned my presidency and no renegade shit like you is going to take it away from me."

"I'd kindly appreciate it if you'd call me by name old man. I'm Rogue Spartan."

"You're in way over your head. My men are everywhere and you'll never get out of here alive."

I laugh, enjoying the verbal threats that Redman is trying to toss my way to throw me off kilter. "Well, from the looks of it I had enough people on my side to get me here into your room. Isn't this the room where you decide the fates of so many people not only in the US, but across the world? Picking winners and losers, trying to change the natural course of man's progression, and overall acting like you're some sort of god when you are in fact the devil."

Redman is standing still and not taking his eyes off me. I am slowly walking toward him and ask, "Do you surrender peacefully or would you rather surrender your life? There may be more pieces of shit around like you to take care of, but that can happen over time. I'm a patient man so one at a time is good enough by me."

In a quick move, Redman grabs something that is on the desk next to him and hurls it at me. It's hard and he connects. I'm stunned by the object and I feel adrenaline rushing through me, trying to help me overcome the pain I feel in my temple. I drop my weapon, but not on purpose. Redman notices and I have no choice but to charge toward him with every bit of force I have. I connect and send him flying back into the ground.

Blood is trickling into my eye as I lock my arms out and try to keep Redman down. He grabs my right wrist with his left hand and flips me over—surprising strength for a seventy year old man. Now he's on top of me and he's trying to strangle me with his hands. "You will not get away with this. You will not ruin what I have created," he's saying through clenched teeth.

I look at his reddening face, turning darker in color the harder he squeezes my throat. I have to do something and I thrust up my palm, delivering a palm heel to his chin. It helps and I notice that he bites his tongue. His eyes start watering and I am able to move my body upward, hitting my head into his nose.

Redman flies back from the connection and I quickly jump up, landing on top of him again. I am so angry and feel so much hatred for this prick right now. I'm staring at him. I don't know if I thought he'd fight back or not any more. I assumed he'd surrender because he's a coward he gets others to do his bidding for him. I'm surprised at how much fight he has in him. He's a monster, that's why.

In another effort to best me Redman's hand comes up and slaps the side of my ear, causing it to pop and start ringing immediately. It's even more challenging to focus now that my left temple is throbbing and my right ear is ringing the way it is. I have to end this and I'm pissed that I underestimated the strength of this man. I try to reach over and grab for my gun so I can just blast him and be done with this. No one is stepping in to help me and that's the way it is to be. Me personally taking on Redman is what gives me credibility. I can do this. I'm so fucking tired right now, but I have to do it. I just have to.

Redman finds a way to pry his knee up between us and jam it into my ribs, causing me to gasp. As he slides out he quickly jumps up and I see blood trickling from his mouth and his eye. He's ruddy looking, but clammy sweaty too. It's like I'm moving in slow motion and it doesn't make sense because everything is unfolding so quickly.

I don't get my gun in time because Redman is able to kick it. I jump up and get ready to lunge for him again. He's backing away from me and going behind a desk so there's something in between us. I try to figure out my best way to get to him with the least amount of energy because I'm getting tapped. If anyone came to help Redman I know I'd be screwed right now. I'm not conditioned for the long haul battle.

It turns out that I don't have to do anything. Redman's eyes suddenly bulge out and he clutches his chest. He's wheezing loudly and I am staring at him, fascinated and appalled in equal measure. I know what this is—it's a heart attack and I can see he's not faking it either. I'd witnessed my grandpa's heart attack when I was little and this looks just like even though my grandpa wasn't bleeding.

I am not sure what to say to him and choose silence. He's meeting his fate and I get to watch. That'll have to be good enough for me. I need to be the better man here and not be tempted to carry on the role of asshole that he's done so masterfully for over twenty years.

A minute later Redman falls to the floor and I can see that his face is already turning a slight shade of blue. He is dead and that is the end. What's next? I'll soon find out.

The door opens and I duck down to pick up my weapon, trying to see who it is there. I see Mr. Richards, followed by Felix and Cal.

"He's dead," I call out and stand up. I look at Cal, almost not recognizing him. Not that I look the same either of course.

"Excellent work," Mr. Richards says. "Now it's time to take care of the last part of your task, Ben and Cal. Felix will escort you to where you need to be now."

I am confused and I know it shows. It's not from the blows I took to my head either. What is going on?

Chapter Twenty-Three: July 4, 2043 at 2:30 p.m.

I am so mad and feeling like a complete jack ass. How could I not see that Felix and Richards were in this together? It makes perfect sense now, but damn it…it's too fucking late now.

Cal and I are sitting in the computer room and Felix is pointing two guns toward our head, sitting on a desk behind us. I know he has them out because I see his reflection in the glass of the computer monitor. I have so many questions to ask, but I know I won't get any answers. Why would he turn like this?

I'd like to talk to Cal also, but I don't even know what to do in this situation. It is not a part of the plan or any scenario I had imagined. Mr. Richards comes into the room with a big smile on his face. I glare at him, knowing it's highly inadequate for what he's just done.

"It's great to have the cooperation of two such highly noted computer hackers here, helping me out."

"Fuck you, Richards," I say.

"That's President Richards and if truth be told, you're probably the one that's fucked, not me. I am in control and everything has gone according to my plan. That's because unlike Redman, I definitely am a smart man."

"I thought you had no aspirations to be President," I spat.

"I didn't need to. The one aspect of the constitution that Redman forgot to change was the one that the VP would take over in case of the President's demise. I'm rather lucky I guess and I have you to thank for killing him, Ben."

"He had a heart attack. That was hardly me."

"But you would have done it. I was watching you on camera and while the old man gave you a rather spirited fight you had a look in your eyes before—a look I've seen many times before."

"And what was that?" I ask.

"The look of a man who was willing to kill to get what he wanted. I guess that makes us rather alike, doesn't it?"

Cal finally interrupts, not even fully able to process what he'd just heard at the moment. "So what do you need us for? Shoot some money into your account, wipe out an identity…what?"

"Oh please, that's child's play, Cal. I need something considerably more complex than that. You and Ben are going to hack into the weapons defense systems and start us a little cyber war. It'll start with other countries currencies dropping, businesses being ruined, and a general loss of ability to operate. What an exciting news day it'll be tomorrow."

"How would that serve you? We could just as easily wipe out all that shit for the US too?" Cal asks.

"You could, but you won't. People are most interesting in making choices that help them self preserve. It's human nature and no place does it better than the United States. That was true long ago and it's true now."

"You think that all the countries will come to you then, asking for your help?" I ask. This is the request of a man with a psychotic based ego if ever there was one. He's fucking insane.

"They will because they will have no choice. Now boys, get to work and don't try anything dumb because Felix won't hesitate to encourage you to do what's right by whatever means necessary. He's pretty intelligent that way, isn't he Ben?" Richards doesn't wait for an answer before giving Felix some orders. "If they don't have these codes broke in three hours time kill them. We'll go to Max and Amy next."

"What?" I scream. I jump up and turn around to look at Felix. "You lied about them being dead?" I feel so low right now and I can't believe what I am going through.

Cal and I have known each other a long time and we know the way each other thinks pretty well. He is not about to do this and I am not either. We start talking in hacker code, the official made-up language of our geek circle, and act as if it's helping us break into the layers of codes that are before us.

The security in the countries is tough and we need to tap into many, including: China, Japan, Russia, Germany, France, United Kingdom, Sweden, India, and Mexico. I am fully aware that these countries make up a total of 98% of the import and export business of the United States, which means that not only will this cause problems for them, but it'll further increase the dependency of people already suffering under the authoritarian ways of the United States. It is a full out global disaster that has more consequences than a war.

"Remember the SOURCE code for the systems initiative actions for strategic monitoring?" Cal asks me.

I pause, not sure where he's going with it. "Yah."

"I think that may work for this initiative as well. Same variables."

I pause again. The SOURCE code for the systems initiative actions for strategic monitoring was one that Cal and Amy had uncovered when they were trying to see what defensive strategies the US had for disarming their own weapons systems.

"So it'd launch the right viruses to cause the mayhem that is desired?" I ask.

"You two are such geek heads," Felix calls out. "Why don't you shut the hell up and get to work. I don't really want to be watching you and listening to your hacking bullshit for the full three hours."

"I'm sure Richards paid you well to serve under him. He's most generous that way."

"I've always been generously compensated by people, RS. How do you think I've been able to help you along the way? Why is it that your mission is suddenly shit now? You got what you set out to do."

"I didn't plan on doing this or answering to Richards, who just may be a more psychotic version of Redman," I say.

I sound calm, but inside my words are pounding in my brain and echoing in my head—which still hurts like hell.

"Well, I told you to be prepared for anything, my friend. Should have listened."

"Will you two shut up. I cannot focus on this crap," Cal says.

"Fine," I reply. "But Cal, do you recall if that sequence had a fast loop trigger? It may help in the process." A fast loop trigger meant that the task that someone wanted you to do virtually would be done for a nano-second before immediately reversing and going back to previous form. In this case, we can make it look like we launched the global economic attack, but it wouldn't last long enough to cause the destruction that Richards is looking for. He wouldn't realize this though because the return circuit would be sent to another computer devise. I just happen to know the perfect computer to handle a fast loop trigger. It's at the bunker in Missouri and definitely built for managing this type of massive information transfer.

I've never had to work so hard and think about what I'm doing in my life. I am trying to break codes for major countries across the world to give the illusion of messing with their economy, while also hacking into the very system I am on to disable to the weapons codes and render the MCU useless. Holy fuck…it doesn't seem real, only I know that it is. Felix casting out condescending comments behind me with a gun in hand, ready to blast me, is a sure indicator. I am not sure if he has one of our guns or a government issued gun either. Our guns, he will still be able to fire when we pull this off. Their guns, he'll be disarmed and well, we'll see what happens. The two guys out there are obviously working with Felix now because they haven't done shit to help us out.

Just as I think this one of them comes in and says that people have been spotted and captured in the west section of the property. My stomach sinks. That's where Gia is. How were they able to capture all of them? It doesn't add up and everything is so fucking messy right now. My stomach sinks at a thought. Is Gia on my side or theirs? Who can I trust? I know that the Anti-Machine has cast their faith in me and they may very well be fighting for me in their villages at this minute. I don't know what's happening anywhere else besides here. There are so many people relying on me and I have to get this done. Deactivating the weapons will make Richards useless, removing the threat he brings.

I shake my head, knowing that I cannot think about Gia now and I put her out of my mind. If we really have something this is what I need to do and if we really don't have something going on, well…this is still what I need to do right now.

Time keeps moving.

"Only thirty minutes left," Felix shouts out.

I am sweating and achy. Cal and I have been typing as quickly as possible for two and a half hours and we are close. Finally Cal whispers, "Trigger loop prepared."

"Five more on the activation sequence," I say. I think we are going to do this. I'm so relieved and know I cannot lose my focus now or even right after. Something else has to happen. I cannot just get up and walk out of here without a care in the world.

Five minutes turns into seven and I finally do it. "Ready," I say to Cal. Felix jumps up and is standing behind me now.

Cal replies with our sync. "3, 2, 1…enter."

I start entering my code in and am suddenly sent flying back from my chair. "I knew you'd try that shit, RS. Nice try, but I stopped you just in time."

"Try what? This is what you wanted, isn't it?" I shout, instantly freaked by not being able to do the weapon deactivation sequence.

"Let's just say I've had some help as to what you are up to."

"What do you mean?" I ask. I really am confused now.

Felix calls out to someone in another room and I don't know to who. "Bring them in."

Cal is looking confused. He doesn't understand all this and he's been locked up with ITC for over a year now. I don't blame him for being confused, but there's no way to start and fill him in on it all. I look over to him and say, "I'll explain later. I need you to trust me."

"Oh yes, trust the Rogue Spartan."

"Rogue Spartan," Cal repeats. He looks at me. "You're the Rogue Spartan? They've been trying to get me to get to you in lock-up. I didn't know. Shit, I'm sorry."

"Don't worry about it now. It's irrelevant and I'll explain later."

"You two are not going anywhere," Richards says. He walks into the room and now I'm really thrown for a loop.

Max and Amy are standing behind him. They appear calm, but it's another unexpected that I couldn't have guessed in my wildest dreams. It's like I'm seeing a ghost because I've mourned their death for so long now, being driven by avenging it for a great deal of my time as the Rogue Spartan.

Mr. Richards is smiling, enjoying the fucking confusion on my face. The prick. He comments, "You know my associates, Max and Amy, yes?"

"What?" Cal replies. I can sense that he's shaking, trying to process this madness. He isn't physically strong at all and even scrawnier than he used to be from being locked up.

"I guess we just didn't think of telling you. It wasn't always easy either, you know," Max says. "Playing the obnoxious dumb boy is so dull in the long haul for someone with talents as advanced as mine."

"Playing," I repeat. This isn't adding up.

"Don't look so dumbfounded, Ben," Amy says. "All that you've become and will become is possible due to this and our guidance ever since we met you in computer school. Nothing is coincidence and you should know that. Yet, you've never grasped that, preferring to be an optimist."

Richard interrupts. "Enough chatting for now. Take them down to lock-up." The guys who I thought were helping me initially in the other room come in and start taking me and Cal down to the lock-up, wherever that is. *They don't seem to want to kill us. At least that's a good thing.*

Chapter Twenty-Four: July 4, 2043 at 5:15 p.m.

Cal and I are escorted to the lock-up area. We don't have any weapons on us and are not handcuffed because it would be pointless. If we act out they can shoot us. They are still carrying activated weapons and at a close range. It doesn't even take a master marksman to nail us, although I know they likely are master shooters.

I'm walking, realizing that I have no idea if these guys know about the activation sequence going full loop or if they were able to stop it. If they stopped it one thing is now started—the economic collapse of the world.

"People will find me, you know," I say. Then I turn to Felix and add, "Not everyone will follow your every word you piece of scum."

Felix looks at me oddly for a moment and I see something in his eyes, something almost sorrowful. Whatever, it's just an act. "Everyone has a price, RS. You're no different."

"Everyone doesn't have a good intention though, a selfless one. I did because I wanted real change in this country."

"You're kidding, right? You took money from Richards to hack just to remain safe. Was that selfless? You dumbed down your knowledge to be closer to Gia. Was that selfless? I don't need to go on because I've proven my point enough."

The guards toss Cal and I into the cell and I notice the lock-up system is a laser and key combination. I am very aware that I am still dressed all in black and my boots protect me against lasers. It may be helpful and I think I have an idea.

Cal and I are now alone, or so it appears. It's doubtful that a camera isn't on us somewhere although I cannot see it above. We casually talk, both understanding the implications of saying too much and I briefly fill him in on everything.

The entire time we're talking and casually looking around. We look at the two beds, sink, and steel toilet in the lock-up cell. I'm assessing what's around me. I end up spotting the camera. It's so tiny and it looks like a speck of rock on the wall. Advanced shit by all standards in this dingy cell.

A guard comes with some food about two hours later. I recognize him from the control room earlier. He is the one that blasted the two and allowed me to advance to Redman. Cal watches him closely too and I can see him memorizing the sequence he inputs on the pad by the movement of his fingers. A whizzing noise sounds as the lasers shut down and the guy enters the cell. Another guy I don't recognize remains outside and watches closely, pointing his weapon at us.

"I want to talk with Amy and Max," I say.

"I'll run it through Felix," the guard says. "No promises." He sounds casual, like he really doesn't care. Maybe that's the problem. People don't care. I'm up against shit like that.

After they're gone Cal and I start eating. We turn our backs to the camera and start to whisper.

"Did you get the laser sequence, Cal?"

"I think so. If they come back again and deactivate it I'll have it."

I lift up my plate and look under it. Taped to the bottom of it is a small scalpel type instrument. It has a very sharp edge on it. I put my finger up to my mouth and point under my plate to Cal. He looks and nods his head. He looks under his plate and finds the same thing. We both remove the sharp tools and Cal slides his into the top of his boot. My boot happens to have a small loop that it slides into easily so I don't have to have it near my skin. Again, I think that it's so planned out and it's damn confusing. If these guys really are spies they should be octagonal agents by now—a double or triple agent would be easy to keep up with, but this…

About an hour later Max and Amy make their way down to see us. Richards is probably looking and listening in, ready to delight in how we have been crossed and screwed by two people we have always thought of as close friends. I know that I am angry about it, but I have to figure something out. Now that I am looking at the two through a different light there are some things I can evaluate to try and determine what the real story is.

I whisper to Cal. "Just follow my lead, okay?"

"Got it."

"Does poor Ben and Cal need some explanations?" Max asks. His voice is different. It sounds the same, but it is not full of the mischievous tone that we've always heard him have.

"What would be in it for you to be on the side of the Machine?"

"Everything is in it for me, for us," Max says. "They gave us life."

"What the hell are you talking about?"

"Without them we couldn't exist. It's just that simple," Amy says. I look in the distance and see the guard, the same one that's been helping me standing guard with someone else. I notice that he is casually undoing a laser sequence for a large door and room next door. I don't know what's going on, but he wants me to see and keep talking.

Amy notices that I'm distracted and turns around to see what I'm looking at, but the guy is done. "You cannot win or get out of here, Ben and Cal. We know your every moves. We've studied you for years and know how you think better than you do."

"Really now," I say. I sit down on the bed and lean over like I'm distraught. I am distraught, but I am trying to get to that little weapon now. I never would have thought that I'd be thinking of delivering a little properly placed stab to people who I'd thought were my friends, but I am now. They aren't my friends and I've already grieved their death. I just did it in reverse order.

Through my peripheral I see Cal scratching his leg and I know he's following suit. I don't know if they can tell or not. I slide the scalpel into my left sleeve, knowing that I'm right handed and will be able to get it out more quickly.

"You know, Amy, I always thought you may have feelings for me. Do you?" I ask. This catches her off guard because it's something that has never been the case or even something that either of us had ever hinted toward. She doesn't know how to respond to this and even her snide snappy comments evade her.

I walk toward her and smile, my hands on my hips. Max starts laughing in the background and before anyone can answer I charge into Max as fast as I can and send him reeling backwards. He lands with a loud bang, almost as if he's a pipe hitting steel or falling on ceramic. It echoes. Why would it echo?

Cal goes toward Amy and tries to hold her back. He isn't strong enough to do it and Max is up. I lunge toward Amy as she tries choking him and pull out the scalpel, stabbing it into her eye. A blue spark flies out and I am thinking fast, trying to process this. They are not real. They are not real.

"Evo-Droids, Cal!" I scream.

"Very good, Ben. It only took you about five years to discover that," Max says, walking toward me and not bothering to hide that he's not human any longer. He is intense and I bolt for the door of the cell. As I swing it open the one guard yells for us to duck. We do and he fires off two shots to Amy and Ben. They startle them and stingy smoke, like what comes from an electrical fire, wafts out.

"You two run. I'll deal with this. Your entourage is waiting by the side door at the end of this hallway. Go now!" Cal and I charge out, not being able to see that well ahead of us. It's dark in the hallways and the lights are as dim as they can be. Everything looks the same.

There's a guard standing there when we reach the end of the hall. He points us left and then turns around. We go left and keep running.

A steel door with a small red light on it shows up in the distance. I large frame is silhouetted in it and it's a frame that I've seen before. It's Fox.

He opens the door. "Good to see you, RS. You're a tough little bastard. Now let's get the hell out of here."

He busts open the door and has his weapon out, ready to fire in an instant if necessary. "Which way?"

"Go to the western part of the woods. The part where Gia was sent to."

"Got it," I say. "Follow me, Cal."

It's about two hundred yards to the western edge of the forest and I am making it okay, knowing that my physical endurance has improved significantly. Cal is having a little different experience and I can hear him wheezing for breath, knowing that he's slowing down his pace. Fox sees it too and grabs him in one swift motion, tossing him across his shoulder and keeps running at pace.

We're almost there. One hundred yards to go.

We get to the clearing just inside the western border of the woods and before I notice anything else I see Richards hanging from a tree, all life thrown from his body. Felix and   Gia   are   standing   nearby.

"I cannot take this fucking shit, Felix. Whose side are you on and what the hell is going on?" I am seething and fed up.

"It was masterful, my friend, but it had to be done," he responds, clapping his hands together loudly. The arrogant shit is giving himself an encore.

Cal looks equally confused and it gets worse when Gia runs up to me and wraps her arms around me, delivering me a huge hug followed by a bigger kiss. " Damn, you made that a close one, Ben. I'm so happy to see you. We've got to get out of here now."

We all begin moving as quickly as possible. Cal is trying his best and I feel bad for him, but I'm damn happy to see him at the same time.

Gia lifts up her wrist and talks into a device on it. "Rogue Spartan on the run. We'll check in when we get to our destination."

Chapter Twenty-Five: July 5, 2043
I am lying in a tent by myself, processing everything in my life. I don't know what's reliable or real. All I do know is that my intentions still remain the same. Yesterday didn't go according to plan, but with the death of two bad Presidents in twenty-four hours there comes the hope of rebirth. This is the chance to move on and I can do so a much wiser man, a more aware man.

As soon as it is possible I shall let the Anti-Machine know that the Rogue Spartan lives on and is willing to fight. As Dr. Jay Secton said, "*For my fellow American's who have kept their constitutional mindset despite the madness, I implore you to be the Rogue Spartan we need in order to change things.*" This may be one quote in which he was wrong. Everyone needs to be the Rogue Spartan and that is how we will win.

www.ingramcontent.com/pod-product-compliance
Lightning Source LLC
Chambersburg PA
CBHW070842120626
46556CB00002B/849